Dukes, Drinks, and Murder

Victoria Parker

Regency Mysteries

Book 1

Jennifer Monroe

Copyright © 2021 Jennifer Monroe

All rights reserved.

This book is a work of fiction. Names, characters, businesses, places, events and incidents are either the products of the author's imagination or used in a fictitious manner. Any resemblance to actual persons, living or dead, or actual events is purely coincidental.

Chapter One

Miss Victoria Parker, known as Vicky to those closest to her, had learned much in her five and twenty years on this earth. Most of what she had come to understand made little sense, in her opinion, but despite her misgivings, there were two points for which she had a decent amount of certainty.

The first was that the accounting office located on Wellington Street in London was always drafty no matter the time of year. Located between a millinery and a butcher's shop, the building had been purchased by her father when she was but ten and she doubted it had ever been repaired since its initial construction.

The large office area with its plush wingback chairs, fine oak end tables, and exquisite leather tomes neatly arranged on a bookcase along one wall, one would believe the professional atmosphere would attract men of the highest caliber.

Which leads to the second certainty that of which Vicky was sure: men of the highest caliber would never accept that Vicky herself was in charge of the accounting business, including the man who sat before her father's desk this morning.

"What a shame your father is now gone," Lord Montague said in a sad tone as he looked over to where she sat, which was a much smaller and less ornate desk allocated for the assistant to the business.

"His understanding of the inner workings of business were unmatched by any other of his position in London. Thankfully, you had the wisdom to appoint the man who studied under him to take his place."

Vicky glanced over at the man in question, Mr. James Kensington, who sat at the large oak desk that had once belonged to her father. James was Vicky's age and a trusted friend. Trusted enough to act the part of the proprietor of the business without the worry he would overstep his place and steal it from underneath her.

Although James did his fair share of the work, and oftentimes more, his role was little more than a facade to keep her father's clients from running to a competitor. For what man would allow a woman to attend to his financial needs? Vicky could not conjure even one name and thus had settled for an imposter to take what should have been her rightful place. It could have been worse, she supposed. At least James was pleasant company.

Offering Lord Montague a polite smile, Vicky hoped to steer the conversation away from her father and toward farewells for the day. "Thank you, my lord—," she began, but the man spoke over her.

"What would people think of the notion of a woman taking over the position that should belong to a man? Surely you would be run out of town! And if I were to be honest, which I am whenever possible, I would understand their outrage. Why, just yesterday, Lord Pernsherm's daughter spoke of an interest in attending university. Her poor mother had such a shock, I fear the woman may never recover." He stood and pulled on the wrinkled sleeves of his coat. Vicky suspected he had worn the garment late into the night if the odor of spirits on his breath was any indication. "Now, Mr. Kensington, if you wish to honor Miss Parker's father, and the young woman herself, you should find her a husband."

Men who spoke of women as if they were not standing in the same room ruffled more than one feather on Vicky's back, but she remained silent. Speaking up would do more harm than good, and her goal was to keep as many clients as she could. She had become well able to hold her tongue, for all too often she was given the opportunity to practice.

James also stood and then winked at Vicky when Lord Montague reached down to retrieve the hat he had dropped. "My lord," he said with a bow, "I hope my work on your ledgers exceeds your expectations. I look forward to seeing you again next month."

Lord Montague snorted. "If you wish me to leave, all you need to do is ask." He turned on his heel and made his way to the front of the office. The panes in the windows rattled to signal his departure.

"I suspect I am nothing more than a decorative piece according to Lord Montague," Vicky said as she took her frustration out on the latch of the door, pinching her finger in the process. "Perhaps next time I shall applaud everything you say. No, I will fall to my knees and proclaim how fortunate I am to be employed by you in my father's business!" She turned and heaved a heavy sigh. "My apologies. I am unsure what came over me."

"You are upset," James said. "And rightly so. You succeed where many have failed and never receive your due praise. In truth, it is I who stands in awe of you. Do you wish me to fall to my knees and thank you?"

As he had done so many times before, James lifted Vicky's spirits. "Do not be silly!" she said, laughing. "You would ruin your trousers and be forced to purchase new ones."

Vicky had known James seven years, and although she had always trusted him in every way, the most peculiar thing occurred. He smiled and ran a hand through his dark hair, which caused Vicky's heart to flutter and her head to become light.

"Vicky?" he asked, his eyes filled with concern. "Are you well?"

"Y-yes," she replied, shaking the haziness from her mind. "Meeting with Lord Montague took more out of me than I realized. There is also the weekend ahead of us. And speaking of such, I must retrieve my bag. The carriage will arrive soon."

Felton Warwick, Duke of Everton, was the most loyal client to Parker Accounting. The old duke had entrusted the accounting of his estate to Vicky's father and had continued to entrust the office with his financial dealings.

Five days earlier, they had been invited to the country estate of the duke for the weekend as a means to celebrate. What was to be celebrated, the invitation did not say, but the fact that she, too, had been asked to attend was extraordinary.

After collecting her carpetbag from the upstairs flat, Vicky joined James at the front door. He stood waiting as patiently as ever, his hand curled in a fist.

At first glance, one might believe him angry and ready to strike, but that was not the case. James had lost two of his fingers at mid-knuckle during a childhood accident. Even after all these years, they brought him a great deal of embarrassment despite the fact she had never heard anyone comment on them.

James took her bag from her. "I have been meaning to ask," he said. "This journey to the duke's will be considered business and not leisure, correct?"

"Yes, of course. Why do you ask?"

He grinned. "To make certain I am paid extra when my wages come in. Perhaps a bonus is in order, as well?"

"As I said," Vicky said hastily, "this is leisure. Think of the fine food and drink you shall receive as your payment for our time there. Now, no more talk of this extra wages nonsense." This, of course, made them both laugh. They spent a great deal of time teasing one another, which helped the workdays pass…perhaps not joyously, but at least they were cheerful.

Then, Vicky found herself staring at his thick hair once again. Why had she suddenly become fascinated with it? And why would she consider the possibility of running her fingers through it?

The door opened and a small head peeked inside. "Miss Parker? Oh, there ye are, miss! I heard ye be askin' after me?"

"I was, indeed," Vicky said with a smile. Percy, a local boy known to every merchant on the street, spent his days running errands in exchange for coin or food. "And what have I told you concerning your hair? If anyone is to take you seriously, you must keep it tidy."

Percy tugged on the ends of his hair that fell well below his ears. "I know it needs cuttin'. Mum says she ain't got the money to buy scissors good enough for cuttin' 'air, and I've been savin' and all, but I'm still a bit short." He clutched a tattered hat in his hands and dropped his gaze. "Forgive me?"

His innocence tore at Vicky's heart, as did his dust-stained cheeks and too-small shoes so in need of mending, his toes poked out the tips.

She squatted down beside him and smiled. "There is nothing to forgive," she said. "The reason I requested your attendance is that I heard it is your birthday. Is that true?"

The boy grinned up at her. "'Tis true, miss. I'm nine years now. Almost a grown man like James."

"I have no doubt you will be as tall as me soon enough," James said, ruffling the boy's hair.

"Now," Vicky said, "I spoke with James concerning a small gift to celebrate this momentous occasion. A growing boy needs so many things, I found it difficult to decide what to give you. Would a turnip be enough?" She paused as if considering the decision. "Yes. I believe a turnip would do nicely."

"Thank ye, miss," Percy replied. "I'll see that Mum adds it to tonight's stew." He glanced around. "Where is it?"

James laughed. "Vicky, do you not think the boy has suffered enough?" He retrieved the gift Vicky had wrapped in brown wax paper and handed it to Percy. "This is from Miss Parker and me."

Percy stared at the package as if it would bite him at any moment.

"Well," Vicky said, "go on. Open it."

He did not hesitate a moment longer and did just that, tossing the paper to the floor. Then he gasped. "A hat!" he exclaimed, his eyes widening. "And a new one at that! Oh, thank you, miss! And thank you, James." He threw his arms first around Vicky and then James. "I'll wear it forever and never take it off! I'm gonna show me mum!"

Before Vicky could respond, Percy was out the door. She sighed as she closed the latch. "The smile on his face," she said in awe. "The boy is so happy."

"You are good to him," James replied as he gathered the paper from the floor. "Your heart is as kind as your father's was."

Adam Parker had been known for giving aid to anyone in need. From local charities to even the town drunk, her father refused no one if he had the money to give. One thing was certain, though. His giving ways, among other wonderful qualities he possessed, had helped shape the woman Vicky was today. Whether she was able to live up to her father's legacy remained to be seen.

James, too, has been a guiding light, she thought. He had been there for her through the worst times, encouraging her during her darkest days. She might have been on the streets without his presence in her life. He might not have had her father's ability for working numbers, but he played his part so well that he could have easily accepted any number of roles in the theater.

"The carriage has arrived," James said, peering out the front window. He collected their bags. "Now, let us see what the duke wants with us."

***

The carriage jostled along the country road, but the soft cushioning on the bench made the journey comfortable. Vicky was not accustomed to riding in a proper carriage – or leaving London for a whole weekend of what she hoped would be repose, for that matter. She could not help but peer out the window like a child on her first outing to see great trees and rolling green landscape pass by them so quickly they seemed a blur.

James had been unusually quiet during the first part of the journey, but now he said, "I believe I may know the reason for the invitation." He was always in search of the whys of the decisions people made, for he believed if one knew a person's motivation, one could predict the outcome of any situation.

Vicky smoothed the skirts of her white and yellow traveling dress, one of the few finely tailored garments she owned. "Is that so?" she asked. "Please tell me because I have yet to make out why I was included on the invitation."

Although the Duke of Everton was a kind man, she had only met him on two occasions. James receiving an invitation was logical as he was the face of the business. But her? Including her made little sense, for she was not one he would call a friend by any definition of the word.

"The duke acquired a new business recently," James said with certainty, "and he wishes us to be there to celebrate. He invited you, as well, for the simple fact that he enjoys your company."

Vicky laughed. "As to the new business, I may agree. However, a man of his wealth acquires new assets weekly. Why invite us now, and in this capacity? I doubt his enjoyment of my company has anything to do with his invitation. It must concern his account with us, for there is no other explanation that makes sense."

The riddle stumped both of them, and James sighed. "He has been married nearly two years now, so it would not concern his new bride."

"That is it!" Vicky said, sitting up in her seat. "The woman is with child." Then she shook her head. "But then why invite me? Or even you, for that matter? We would not be included in such an important announcement."

"Surely it has nothing to do with the rumor…" James paused. "No, that could not be it. Forget I mentioned it."

Vicky leaned forward and set a steady gaze on her friend. "What rumor?"

"The one I started concerning you," he replied. "I let word slip of the cruel conditions in which I am forced to work. Surely word has reached the duke, and he has taken pity on me. Tonight we will celebrate your journey to the gallows for your mistreatment, and dare I say neglect, of me." He grinned at Vicky.

"James Kensington!" Vicky admonished, but she struggled to maintain a stern countenance. "I cannot believe you would do such a thing. After all this time, I thought you were my friend."

Concern etched James's features. "I will always be your friend, Vicky. You know that."

Vicky smiled and nodded. "Yes, I do know that."

An awkward silence fell between them and they turned their attention to the passing landscape.

"Whatever this journey brings," James said, "I do hope it does not rain. Rain always ruins a good weekend."

"I agree," Vicky replied, not knowing that rain would have nothing to do with what would ruin their visit.

Chapter Two

Stanting Estate was located just over an hour's journey outside of London, and upon arrival to the great house, Vicky was immediately impressed. The gray stone gave the home a dull appearance, but the presence of green ivy climbing the walls and flowerbeds filled with purple and yellow flowers surrounding the great structure, the estate came to life. The steps that led to the portico could have easily held a dozen men shoulder to shoulder. Even the stable, located behind the house, was easily thrice the size of any estate she had seen.

Vicky was uncertain if she should enter through the main door or that of the servants, but she had been invited as a guest. Therefore, she knocked on the grand front door, and a butler answered. "Miss Parker, Mr. Kensington," he said as if they had met before, "His Grace awaits you in the sitting room." The man bowed before extending his arm and moving aside to indicate that Vicky and James were to enter.

The foyer did not disappoint. Massive tapestries hung from the walls depicting images from the Far East. Tall white vases with gold and blue etchings stood on dark oak tables, holding carefully arranged flowers. It appeared the duke spared no expense in his choice of décor.

"James," Vicky whispered, unable to keep the awe from her voice, "the chandelier. Is it not magnificent?"

James nodded. "It is," he whispered back. "Do you think it is new?"

"His Grace inherited the chandelier from his father," the butler replied as if they had asked him directly, "who inherited it from his father before him. For four generations, it has been an integral part of this estate, and I suspect it will remain for another four. This way, please."

They followed the butler past a grand staircase and down a hallway adorned with paintings of various landscapes and tapestries until they arrived at a massive set of double doors. The sitting room had blue wallpaper with white floral patterning and gold and red panels, thick red drapes pulled back from tall windows, and gold and blue furniture.

The butler announced them to the half a dozen or so people in the room. The men stood, including the duke, and the women turned to stare at them.

"Come in, come in," the duke said, smiling. "No need to be shy."

Vicky dropped into a deep curtsy, surprised at the courtesies shown to one of her station. "We are honored to be here, Your Grace."

"The honor is all mine," the duke replied, catching Vicky off-guard. To have him make such a statement in the company of his peers made her stomach tighten into knots. She could imagine the thoughts of the better guests at this very moment.

Why would His Grace speak to this lesser woman as if she were our equal? the lady with the dark hair carefully piled high in an elegant chignon likely was thinking. Her penetrating blue eyes held little warmth.

Who does she think she is putting on airs? This thought Vicky imagined came from the younger lady, her blond curls framing a perfect, doll-like face.

"Please, sit," the duke said. "We shall begin our celebration shortly."

Smiling, she took a seat on a long couch where another man already sat, James sitting beside her on the end.

The wrinkles around the duke's eyes deepened as he requested everyone's attention. "Everyone is now here," he said. "Each of you was invited for a celebration, although none was told what we would be celebrating, including my wife."

He turned to smile at the blond lady, who was nearly fifty years younger than him. "Charlotte, I know you have been curious, as I am sure all of you are."

The duchess nodded, as did the other guests, including Vicky and James. Most were leaning forward as if each word the duke spoke held the key to life itself.

"When I was a boy," the duke continued, "I dreamed of sailing to distant lands. Of meeting other people and understanding the ways of those who are different from myself. I do not wish to be known simply as a duke but as a renowned explorer, as well. It is for that reason I have booked passage to India."

The duchess raised her glass, a smile crossing her lips. "What a wonderful holiday we shall have!" she said. "Imagine the sights we shall see and the people we will meet! What wonderful tales we will bring home with us."

"It will not be a holiday, my dear," the duke said. "My plan is to live there indefinitely."

This brought about a collective gasp of surprise from the onlookers, as the duchess gaped at her husband. "Indefinitely?" she choked.

"But Your Grace," Lord William Gerard, a baron in his mid-thirties with a long but slightly upturned nose and impeccable clothing, said, "surely you cannot believe such a move would be practical. What about the acquisition of the mines in the North? If word gets out that you are leaving, the deal will surely fail."

The duke sighed. "That no longer matters to me anymore, Gerard. I am sorry, but I will be withdrawing my offer to invest in that venture. My days of postponing adventures so I can deal in business are over."

Lord Gerard leaped from his seat. "May I assume I will have your blessing to continue this deal with the marquess, then?"

"George?" the duke said, laughing outright. "I am afraid he is not quite ready to engage in such dealings just yet. One day, he will take my place as duke, and then he will be able to pursue such matters, but he may not do so until then." He turned a piercing gaze on his son. "He still has too much to learn. If he learns any of it at all."

The room fell silent and the atmosphere grew cold. Vicky glanced at the marquess. Not yet thirty, Lord George Warwick hung his head and looked at the floor. His wife, Lady Lavinia Warwick, whispered to him, but he merely shook his head at whatever she was insisting.

Out of the shadows emerged a man Vicky recognized instantly. Had she realized that Richard Kent would also be in attendance, she would have taken more time to consider accepting the invitation. Never had she met a man so vile and so outrageous in his behavior. Being in the same room with him made her feel ill.

"I am sure His Grace will settle business matters with each of us before the night ends," Mr. Kent said. "We should be spending this time celebrating his newfound sense of adventure and not pressing him in the direction we wish him to take." He lifted his glass. "May he find whatever it is he goes in search of."

"Thank you, Kent," the duke said. "We shall speak after dinner. In fact, I plan to speak with each of you individually at some point after we finish eating. I would suggest keeping your schedules open."

A sudden pang in Vicky's stomach made the idea of eating uncomfortable. Did he plan to inform her that he would be turning elsewhere for his accounting?

No, that made no sense. Perhaps he would request that she, and James, of course, keep a close eye on his ledgers in his absence. Although the younger Warwick was recognized as one of the kindest men in London, he was also sadly known to be one of the most gullible, as well. It was no wonder his father refused to trust him with any business dealings until the day he had no choice.

"I, for one, wish you nothing but the best," Lord Warwick said as if his father's words had not affected him in the least. "I believe I speak for everyone when I say we drink to your success in this new adventure in life." He stood. "Let us go around the room and say a few words about my father!"

This brought about an eruption of overindulgent smiles – and a great deal of crowing and adulation from the guests.

Lord Gerard began, his arrogance thicker than the storm clouds gathering on the horizon. "May you increase in happiness and wealth," he said, raising his glass, "both of which I have no doubt you will see great success! For there is none more intelligent, more knowledgeable…"

One by one, each person spoke, adding grander gestures than the person before him or her, and the duke responded with polite acknowledgment.

Vicky prayed her words would not fall flat, for speaking before large, or even small, groups of people had always been a struggle. It was as if the words formed in her brain but became stuck in her throat when she went to say them aloud.

"Vicky," James whispered.

All eyes were on her. She tried to bring moisture back to her mouth, her heart racing as if she were a rabbit and the others dogs in pursuit. She was unsure how, but she managed to blurt out a quick toast.

Chapter Three

"Perhaps you will see an elephant," Vicky muttered angrily as she stood beside James in the garden. "Of all the foolish things I could have said, I had to say that!"

She was surprised the duke had not thrown her out on her ear! The others, including James, had wished the couple good luck, new fortune, or other words worthy of the ears of a duke. Vicky had spent so much time worrying about what she would say that she blurted out the first thing that came to mind, leaving the room in complete and utter silence. Except for the snickers that had followed, of course.

Thankfully, the duke gave the same polite smile he had given the others.

"Mr. Kensington?"

They turned to see the butler standing on the veranda. "Yes?" James replied.

"Dinner is served."

"Thank you." James offered Vicky his arm. "Well, shall we go inside?"

Vicky sighed. "Just kick me if it seems I will make an idiot of myself again, will you?"

"Absolutely," he said with a grin. "I have no qualms about kicking you if the need arises."

Giving him a playful slap on the arm, she allowed him to lead her back inside and to the dining room.

Vicky was immediately impressed, not only with the fine table settings and the silver candleholders but also with the two massive paintings that hung from opposite walls. They depicted ships at sea, and the detail was so stunning, Vicky felt as if she were there.

"They have always inspired me to travel abroad," the duke said as he approached Vicky. "I have always wanted to sail beyond the edges of the known world and lay eyes on creatures never before seen or written about in books."

Vicky offered him a polite smile, though she did not speak. She had made that mistake earlier and would not do so again.

"Please, have a seat," the duke said. "The footmen will bring out our food soon enough."

As she and James made their way to the last two empty chairs, Vicky could feel the eyes of the other guests on them. When she had first realized that Mr. Kent was in attendance, she had worried she would be forced to sit beside him. Thankfully, she sat beside the marchioness instead. The fact Mr. Kent sat across from her, however, was still much too close for her liking.

Once everyone was seated, the duke rang a tiny bell, and a line of footmen came through a door in the far corner, each carrying a heavily ladened tray. The first course consisted of a soup Vicky later learned was artichoke – she had never eaten artichoke in anything, including soup, and found it quite tasty.

As they ate, the duke discussed his upcoming travels with gusto. Vicky glanced at the duchess and was shocked to see her smiling at Lord Gerard. To surprise her further, although he nodded from time to time as if acknowledging what the duke had said, the baron's eyes seemed to be on the duchess. More particularly on the plunging neckline of her gown!

"I am unsure if we will host a party before Charlotte and I leave," the duke said, causing the duchess to glance up at him. "Yet the idea of seeing the envy on the faces of my foes is quite tempting."

This seemed to please the duchess, for she replied, "Then allow me to plan the finest meal for that party. That way their misery is served on a full stomach."

"Your Grace," Lady Warwick said as she dabbed at the corner of her mouth with a serviette, "I would be more than happy to plan the festivities. A party of such importance calls for a lady with a great deal of experience. No offense to you, of course, Charlotte." She patted the duchess on the hand. "It is just that I have planned so many parties, I could do so in my sleep, and let us be honest, you lack a sense of...shall we say culture? When it comes to planning such important gatherings."

Vicky stared in amazement at the audacity of the marchioness to insult the wife of her father-in-law. Granted, the duchess was much younger than Lady Warwick. It appeared the marchioness had failed to release the responsibilities of the household duties to the woman who should have held control over them upon marrying the duke.

Rather than admonishing Lady Warwick, the duke simply sipped at his soup and then smiled. "I must admit that your attention to detail pleases me, Lavinia." Then he frowned. "Perhaps my son should take lessons from you on how to fulfill his duties."

Lady Warwick smiled broadly, but her husband dropped his head as if he were a child caught in some sort of mischief. The duchess, however, glared first at the duke and then at the marchioness.

Vicky's heart raced. Would the family openly fight while entertaining guests? No, of course not. They were far above airing their petty squabbles in front of their peers.

Taking another sip of the marvelous soup, Vicky turned to tell James just how much she was enjoying it only to see Mr. Kent grinning at her. Then he had the audacity to wink at her! If that was not terrible enough, he followed that with a raising of both eyebrows twice in quick succession.

She was so offended, the spoon fell from her fingers, dropping into the bowl with a loud plink that made her ears ring.

"Miss Parker?" the duke asked with concern. "Is there a problem with your soup?"

Every eye was on Vicky, and she could feel the heat build in her cheeks. Mr. Kent chuckled softly and Lord Gerard rolled his eyes as if to say, *What did you expect of a woman so far beneath us?*

"Not at all, Your Grace," Vicky replied, her mind struggling to devise a suitable excuse for her disruption. "My arm simply grew tired, is all." She glanced around the table and swallowed hard. "That is...or rather..."

She closed her eyes. Surely she had made enough of a fool of herself once again. Now the duke would realize his error in inviting her to such an important gathering and ask that she be escorted from the premises!

"If I may say so, Your Grace," James said, smiling, "the ships depicted in those paintings. Do they belong to you?"

The duke looked up at the paintings in question and smiled. "They are. In fact, the one on the left..."

Vicky sighed in relief as the duke went on to explain the origin of the artwork and why he had it commissioned, but she did not pay attention. As he had done so many times before, James had come to her rescue. Perhaps she should see he received a small increase in wages, after all.

The marquess coughed, which drew a look of disapproval from his wife. Mr. Kent rose from the table as if he were simply sitting in a public house and left the room.

This certainly is an odd assortment of people, Vicky thought as she continued with her soup. Did the duke notice that his very young wife was sharing in secretive smiles with the baron? Vicky had never been one for gossip nor idle speculation, but it appeared the two were on more intimate terms than what was appropriate.

Then there was the duke's son, a marquess with a wife who treated him more like a child than a husband who would rise to become the next Duke of Everton.

"You are eating far too quickly," the marchioness snapped at one point only to say later, "Do not dawdle, George. You do not want everyone waiting for you to finish eating before the next course is brought out, do you?" At one point Vicky heard her say, "Look at your father when he speaks to you!" followed several moments later by "Why do you stare at him so?"

Mr. Kent returned during the fish course, and Vicky could feel his eyes boring into her. Yet, she refused to give him the satisfaction of returning his gaze.

"Excuse me," Lady Warwick said, a finger on her temple. "I must go for a headache powder." When several chairs scraped the floor, she quickly added, "No need to get up on my account. I will not be gone long."

Indeed, she returned several minutes later to a heated conversation about how best to deal with the dropping prices of copper.

Then Lord Warwick cleared his throat. "It is my hope that in my father's absence I will expand the family fortune by dabbling in several business ventures that have been presented to me in recent months."

The marchioness clicked her tongue. "I believe your father has expressed quite clearly that he wishes you to wait until you are more prepared, my love. Would it not be best if we adhere to his wishes? Do you not agree, Your Grace?"

The old duke nodded. "Indeed. That is precisely what I wish. And I expect my wishes to be upheld. You will have plenty of time to do what you want once I am dead and buried."

All conversation ended as the next course was served: duck with roasted potatoes drizzled with a thick wine sauce. Once the footmen stepped away, the duke began to speak again.

"When we have finished with dinner, I would like us to enjoy a few drinks in the sitting room. I have scheduled private meetings with each and every one of you, but that will happen much later. You will be given the time of your scheduled appointment after we have finished our drinks." He became serious. "I expect you to be on time. I will not suffer tardiness."

Lord Gerard frowned. "What matters will we discuss?" he asked.

"You will know in due time, Gerard," the duke growled. "Now, no more talk of business. Let us finish our meal in peace."

Vicky waited until several others had begun eating before picking up her fork. She did not want to run the risk of embarrassing herself again.

Like the others, she was curious what the duke wished to discuss with a spinster who was believed to be nothing more than the assistant to the man who had taken the place of her father.

***

"Are you still fretting over your earlier toast?" James whispered as Vicky followed him out into the gardens. "You really should not waste so much time on such things."

He was right, of course. She had spent the entire time the party shared in drinks after dinner worrying about how silly her tongue could be. When the duke noticed she had not done more than sip her sherry, he asked her if she was unwell, to which she assured him she was not. She continued to focus her thoughts on that one slip of the tongue, however. It really was a waste of her time, but she could not stop herself.

"There are worse things you could have said, you know," James said. "You could have asked if he had an extra ticket for passage and invite yourself along." This made her giggle. "At least you can hope the marquess found it amusing and will continue using your services for his accounting once his father is gone."

Vicky sighed. "You are right. It could have been much worse." She glanced around to see if anyone was close enough to overhear. The area was empty. "But why is it that every time I speak to more than two people at one time, my tongue ties itself into knots? I was not giving a speech to soldiers before the war or advising the King of matters important to the crown. I was giving a simple toast!"

"You are overthinking," James replied, "a malady with which I have a tendency to suffer." Her surprise at his admission must have shown, for his face reddened to his ears. "You look at me as if I just confessed to murder."

"It is just that I never thought of you as one who struggled with something as mundane as overthinking. May I ask what brings about your form of 'malady' as you put it?"

James placed his damaged hand behind his back. "It is of no importance," he replied, giving more of an answer in his actions than he realized. "We have a wonderful weekend of leisure ahead of us. Let us enjoy it."

Vicky smiled, but her heart felt a pang of hurt for him. She knew he worried about his hand and the looks he often received because of the missing portions of his fingers. With children, she could understand how curiosity might overtake manners, but much too often it was adults who stared in open wonderment.

"Indeed," she agreed. "And this is a weekend of leisure we have both earned. I understand that Lord Warwick is leading the fishing expedition tomorrow. Will you be attending?"

James grinned. "I would never pass up the chance to enjoy a favored pastime with a future duke. Plus, I may be able to use the opportunity to learn if any of the other guests are in need of accounting services."

"As long as Richard Kent is not one of those guests," Vicky whispered. "I find the man insufferable and want nothing to do with him. Even if he was the only client willing to give us the time of day, I would not accept his accounts. More than likely, we would find ourselves in prison, or worse, hanging from the gallows!"

Stories about Mr. Kent did not sit well with Vicky. She had heard he dabbled in illegal activities and was known to swindle widows. Whether or not it was true made little difference to her, but those reasons would make it easy for her to refuse him.

"As I fish, you will spend the day embroidering with the duchess and marchioness," James teased. "A most exhilarating day, comparable only to exploring India."

Vicky could not help but laugh. She despised the mundane task of embroidery with a passion. It was such a trivial dalliance when there were more interesting and useful pastimes to be had, such as reading or visiting a museum. What could a lady possibly learn by pushing a needle and thread through a swatch of cloth?

James reached into his pocket and pulled out a watch. "It is time to speak with the duke," he said. "Would you like me to wait here for you?"

Vicky shook her head. "No, that is not necessary. Go on to bed and I will speak to you in the morning." Both of them had been surprised when James's name had not been added to the list of people with whom the duke wanted to speak. Did he know the truth about their business? Apparently so.

James went inside as Vicky took a moment to study the sky. What did the duke wish to discuss with her? She felt a twinge of sadness knowing it would likely be the last time they would speak before he left. Although he was a duke and as such spoke highly of himself, he was a kind man. The few times he had come to her father's office, he had always greeted her where so many chose to ignore her.

Which once again brought about the question as to why he would wish to speak to her now.

"No more talks of elephants," Vicky whispered to herself as she made her way back inside the house. "Do not embarrass yourself again!"

The house was eerily quiet as she made her way down the hallway that led to the study. A clock struck midnight, and she hurried her steps so she would not be late. At the door, she drew in a deep breath and stepped inside. Any sensibility left her and she began speaking at once.

"Your Grace," she said, "I hope I am not late. And I would like to apologize further for my words earlier."

The duke sat at his desk, and Vicky tilted her head. His eyes were wide, his mouth hung open, and he held a pen in his hand. The man appeared in shock, and Vicky realized why.

She dropped into a deep curtsy. "Your Grace, forgive me!" She lowered herself so close to the floor that she nearly toppled over. "I have embarrassed myself in your presence thrice this evening, and I promise it will not happen again!"

She waited for a response, and when none came and she could no longer hold that pose, she stood once more, straightening her back into a perfect posture.

Still he did not speak.

Should she sit? No, that was rude and would earn another tally of embarrassment. Instead, she approached the desk, her eyes focused on the tips of her slippers, and awaited the reprimand that was sure to come. With each passing second, her fear mounted. Was he attempting to control his rage before he spoke?

Still, nothing came.

She peeked through her lashes. A bottle of brandy and two glasses sat on the desktop, one of which was empty. Was the other for her?

Of course not, you fool! What man of the aristocracy, let alone a duke, drank brandy with a woman who was nothing more than the assistant to an accountant?

Then her eyes fell on the parchment in front of him. Something was scrawled across it, and she strained to see what it was without him noticing. All she could make out was a single word.

Betrayed.

Vicky's heart thudded in her breast as she looked up at the duke's face once more. The expression he had worn on her arrival had not changed. In fact, it seemed worse, for his eyes were frozen not in shock but rather in terror.

Covering her mouth lest she scream, Vicky slowly backed away.

Please tell me he is not dead!

She continued to walk backward, her eyes not leaving the duke, until she bumped into something. Or rather, someone.

Turning around, she was met with a mischievous grin.

"Miss Parker," Richard Kent said, his eyes moving from her to the duke and back again, "if I may be so bold to ask. What are you doing here?"

Chapter Four

"Mr. Kent!" Vicky croaked. "I was merely…that is, the duke! He is dead!"

Mr. Kent nodded as if she had told him it was raining as they stood beneath the droplets. "Allow me to see for myself before we announce the death of a man who has fallen asleep." He walked around the desk and leaned in close to the duke.

Is the man mad? Vicky thought. *Why is he looking at him in that way?*

"Come here, Miss Parker," Mr. Kent said after several moments had passed.

Vicky swallowed back bile. "I-I do not think it wise," she stammered.

"The dead cannot hurt you," Mr. Kent said with a small smile. "It is only the living about whom you should worry. Now, come here and have a look."

With heavy steps that felt as if she were walking through mud after a terrible storm, Vicky rounded the desk and stood beside Mr. Kent.

"The word 'betrayed' is written here," he said. "Now, do you see the two glasses?"

Vicky nodded. "Yes. What of them?"

Mr. Kent pointed at the duke's face. "The corner of the man's lips has a strange tint of green, and no brandy contains such color. It is clear the man has been poisoned."

If the situation had not been so dire, Vicky would have laughed. He truly believed her an imbecile! "Thank you, Mr. Kent," she said dryly, "but I had already come to that conclusion myself. The note, the drink, and his lack of breath all led to that conclusion."

"Now, Miss Parker, we find ourselves in quite a quandary, do we not? And because we have shared in such an intimate finding, let us forgo the formalities. My name is Richard, why not address me as such? And may I call you Victoria?" Vicky went to refuse, but he continued on as if she had no objection. "Now that formalities are out of the way, I must summon the constable. Yet, before I go, I have one question. Was it you who poisoned the duke?"

"I?" Vicky replied with a gasp. Could he be any more offensive? "I would never do such a thing! How dare you make such an accusation!"

Richard did not seem ruffled by her adamant refusal. "Unless the man poisoned himself, who else would I suspect? After all, you were the only other person in the room when I entered." He placed his hands on his thighs as if he had solved the most ancient of mysteries on earth.

Vicky, however, clenched her jaw. How dare he insult her! "Now, you see here, Richard."

Richard? Speaking his given name left a bitter taste on her tongue. Yet, she had no doubt he would address her as Victoria even if she denied giving him permission. But how they addressed one another was a problem to be solved later.

"For a man who steals from widows and devises schemes for the foolish, I should not be surprised that you would choose to accuse me. I see now that it was you who killed the duke."

She began to pace, her hands behind her back as she was wont to do while working out a difficult problem. Her father had told her on more than one occasion she would wear out the floorboards if she were not careful.

"It is quite simple to deduce, really. There is a decanter of brandy and two glasses, a drink typical of men more often than women.

Therefore, I believe it was you who poisoned him! Now you have this feeble excuse of going for the constable when in fact you want to make your escape, but you likely had this all planned out from the beginning."

Her pacing increased. "Yes! In the shadows you hid, waiting for the duke to perish. It was your luck that I entered the room, and therefore you are able to place the blame on me. However, I assure you that I will not be accused of a crime you committed. Not this crime nor any others you may have carried out!"

Vicky was panting by the time she finished her tirade – she had no doubt it was a tirade — and although she felt better, she worried that Richard would accuse her still. Who better to blame than a spinster of the working class? It was diabolical and yet brilliant at the same time.

For a moment, she imagined a barrister staring down at her, pronouncing her sentence. Then she would be led away to the gallows. Angry mobs would throw stones at her as their vile curses filled the air. James would be there to support her as he always had, but his mournful expression would push her over the edge. No, she would insist he not attend her execution.

"An interesting theory," Richard said. "But I have no reason to murder the duke. Tell me, what were you doing here with him alone?"

"He requested I meet with him at midnight," she replied. "I was here but two minutes before you showed yourself." She paused. "Where were you hiding, by the way?"

"I was not hiding at all," he replied. "I simply walked through the door. But you? You were in the presence of a dead man for two minutes." He lifted the glass that still contained brandy toward the window as he peered through the liquid. "Tell me, Victoria, do you practice witchcraft?"

Vicky raised her chin and glared at him. "I will not be insulted a moment longer," she said. "First you accuse me of murder and then witchcraft, but I assure you I am guilty of neither. Why would you ask such a question?"

Richard replaced the glass on the desk and turned to face her. "Do not be upset by my inquiry. Our beloved duke was involved in the dark arts. Quite heavily, in fact. Perhaps a fellow member of his..." He paused. "Would it still be referred to as a coven if it is a group of men? Well, it does not matter. What I am saying is that maybe one of his group members murdered him."

Never having heard such nonsense, Vicky rolled her eyes. Most women would be easily diverted by such nonsense, but Vicky was not like most women. She had spent too many years listening to the conversations of men to be led astray by such hogwash.

"I am well aware that your mention of this mumbo jumbo is nothing more than a feeble attempt to distract me," she said. "But it only brings more suspicion upon yourself. Witchcraft? And to say the duke practiced or was somehow involved with it? I have never heard such rubbish." Her frustration rising, she took a step toward him. "I will ask you again. What brought you here at such a late hour?"

"Perhaps my mention of the dark arts was a bit far-fetched," he said, chuckling. "However, I was asked to come at five minutes past midnight, and I am one to never be late to any appointment."

Vicky regretted revealing to this man the time given to her. Clearly he was lying, for why would the duke schedule meetings a mere five minutes apart? Then again, how long did it take for a duke to sack his accountant?

"I still do not know why he wished to speak to me," Richard continued. Then he grinned. "Perhaps he wished to play matchmaker."

"That insult is worse than if it had been me you accused of witchcraft!" Vicky snapped. She drew in a deep breath to calm herself. Anger would get her nowhere. "Why were you invited this weekend?"

"I am afraid it is a personal matter," he replied. "If I were to reveal the truth it would only bring shame to our beloved duke. Now, since you believe I wish to make my escape, I will send a servant for the constable rather than go myself. Does that ease your suspicions of me?"

Nothing short of a confession by the true murderer would ease her suspicions of this man. Even if that were to happen, she suspected him of too many other dastardly deeds to make her trust him in the slightest.

He went to move past her, and she grabbed him by the arm. She had yet to know for certain his opinion concerning her guilt! "What will you tell the constable when he arrives?"

Richard glanced down at her hand, his blue eyes twinkling, and she pulled away. "Why, the truth, of course. Both of us arrived at the same time to speak to the duke. And both of us found him dead."

"That is not the truth!" Vicky whispered. "In fact —"

"The facts are quite clear, Miss Parker. Although I do not believe you killed him, the constable and Warwick — the son, that is — will believe you did. After all, you were alone with him when I arrived. You should be thanking me for my willingness to lie on your behalf."

Vicky ground her teeth. "Not for any noble reason," she said. "But rather to keep suspicion off yourself."

"That may be partly true," Richard said. "But I do it because I must learn who did kill the duke. It is important to me that the person pays dearly for it."

"I do not understand," Vicky said, frowning. "Why is it so important to you? Surely the two of you were not that close."

Richard stopped at the door and turned back to face her. "Because he owed me a debt," he replied, looking past Vicky toward the duke. "And now I will never be able to collect on it."

***

Vicky woke the following morning just as the sun rose, her eyes burning after only two hours of sleep. Despite the fact she had come close to crawling up the stairs to the room assigned to her, sleep had alluded her for several hours. How she had managed to fall asleep at all after what had transpired the night before was beyond her.

What she had hoped was to wait for the constable to arrive, but Richard had convinced her that she should get as much rest as she could before the inquest began. Now she was glad he had. Even two hours was better than none, and she needed all her faculties for what would take place today.

She chose a dark blue dress with intricate white embroidery around the neckline, which was tasteful or prudish depending on how one viewed such things. There were no men to entice here, or anywhere, nor would there ever be if she had anything to say about it.

Vicky was glad to be a spinster. Such a title bestowed upon a woman brought about scorn and ridicule from others, but James and Laura who ran the millinery beside the accounting office were the only peers she had whose opinions mattered. Neither of them would look at her as less than a woman because of the choices she had made.

As she left her room, Vicky considered going first to the room assigned to James to inform him what had occurred the night before but instead decided to make her way to the drawing room. James would find out soon enough.

When she neared the door to the sitting room, an unfamiliar voice came to her ears.

"And where is this Miss Parker?" the man asked. "I wish to begin the inquest and do not wish to repeat myself." That had to be the constable Richard had sent for.

Immediately, Vicky knew her life was over. The constable had arrived and was ready to lead her to the gallows. She glanced down. At least she would look presentable for death in her new dress.

She entered the room and seven sets of eyes stared at her — those of James, Richard Kent, Lord and Lady Warwick, the duchess, Lord Gerard, and an older man with thick white eyebrows and a paunch of a stomach that threatened to pop the buttons on his coat. Why had no one come to wake her sooner?

"Miss Parker, I presume?" the man with the thick eyebrows said.

"Yes," she replied, unsure from where the ability to speak came. "I am she."

"I am Constable Cogwell. I understand from Mr. Kent that you and he stumbled upon the duke late last night?" Vicky nodded. "Did you witness anyone else leaving the study?"

Before she could reply, Richard said, "I already told you there was no one else, Cogwell. The lady is apparently still in shock, and such questioning is redundant."

Constable Cogwell snorted in clear offense but then directed his questions to the duke's son, Lord Warwick. "My lord…Oh my, I suppose we should begin addressing you as Your Grace now that you are the new duke."

Lord Warwick frowned. "No. I refuse to accept the title until we learn who murdered my father – no matter what custom dictates. Until then, I am simply the Marquess of Warwick. It is only right."

Vicky pursed her lips in thought. Was the request a way to hide his guilt or was he truly being charitable to his father's memory?

Lady Warwick gasped. "You dare to question a marquess, the man who will become the new Duke of Everton?" she demanded. The woman had dark hair, deep blue eyes, and wore the most exquisite green dress Vicky had ever seen. "George was asleep, as any sensible man would be at that late hour. I, of course, was with him and can attest to that."

Lord Warwick patted her hand. "Lavinia, my love, do not be angry at the man. He is merely doing his job. An inquest such as this will require many questions, which will lead to answers I am sure the good constable will use to learn who committed this terrible deed."

The constable, clearly pleased by the marquess's explanation, adjusted his trousers. "Thank you, my lord. It is my duty to find the murderer, and I shall do so within no more than a few minutes."

Vicky had to hide a smile. Constable Cogwell alluded to a quick mind, yet his disheveled appearance led her to believe he might have exaggerated. Only time would tell if he spoke the truth.

The constable turned to James. "And you, sir?"

"I?" James asked. "Why, I was asleep."

"Very well," Constable Cogwell replied as he made a note on a tiny pad. "And to —"

"My husband is dead," the duchess said, drawing all eyes to her. "And now I am burdened not only with planning his funeral, but I must also endure the gossip of the ton, as well. Why he chose to die before we left for India is beyond me, but I was asleep in my room dreaming of the new life we would lead together." She sniffled and dabbed her nose with a handkerchief, although her eyes lacked even a hint of the glisten of unshed tears. She turned to Richard. "Thank you, Mr. Kent, for not waking me to give me the news and allowing me to rest. I would never have been able to endure this day if you had. It is difficult enough as it is."

"Whatever I can do to serve you, Your Grace," Richard said with a bow of his head.

Vicky was stunned when Richard flashed the duchess a tiny smile, which the duchess returned. Not a friendly smile but rather a conspiratorial one.

She was not given time to consider this, for Lord Gerard rose from his chair. A handsome man with a chiseled jawline and blond hair that fell in waves around his ears, he was rumored to be rather friendly with the women. After the way he ogled the duchess at dinner the previous night, the rumors were likely true.

"We have all indicated that we were asleep when this tragedy struck," the baron said. "Therefore, good constable, will you keep us here until we starve in hopes one of us will confess? Or will you allow us to break our fast and gain nourishment?"

"My apologies," Lord Warwick said, standing. "Father wished you all to have an enjoyable and leisurely weekend, and I believe he would have wanted us to see his plans realized. I suggest we begin with a wonderful breakfast before we engage in activities for the day. Constable Cogwell, may I have food brought to you?"

"I suppose a bite or two will not get in the way of my inquest," the constable replied as he smacked his lips in anticipation. "And now that I have heard everyone's accounts of their whereabouts last night, I now realize that my inquest may take longer than I first expected."

Vicky sat dumbfounded. The duke had been murdered during the night, yet his son was more concerned with playing host? The attitude of those experiencing a loss was strange indeed. Where was the mourning? The heart-wrenching stories of a son who had lost his father? The distressed cries of anguish of a young bride turned widow?

These questions, as well as others, ran through Vicky's mind as Lord Warwick explained the day's activities, including the fishing expedition that had been planned for the men.

As they made their way to the dining room, Vicky glanced at Richard. Why had he insisted on protecting Vicky, even when the man knew she detested him? And even more importantly, why was the duchess still smiling at Richard?

Chapter Five

Breakfast consisted of a choice of poached eggs, porridge with dried fruit, a variety of cakes, and several hot drinks. No sooner had they begun to eat than the duke's son heaved a heavy sigh, drawing all attention to him.

"I always enjoyed eggs in the morning with Father," he said. "Now I will be left to eat them alone." He smiled at his wife. "Lavinia is not fond of eggs, nor is her mother. Even her grandmother loathes them. It is quite peculiar if one thinks about it."

"There is nothing peculiar about not liking eggs," Lady Warwick retorted with such frustration, Vicky wondered if the woman's head would explode. "For a man who wishes to please everyone, you would think I would receive the same courtesy. I do not like eggs, nor shall I ever."

"I am sorry, my love," her husband lamented. "I meant no insult."

The marchioness returned his smile. "Of course, George. I know you meant nothing by your words. I suppose it is the loss of your father that has us on edge. We are in mourning, after all, and—"

"Enough!" the duchess snapped as her utensils clinked on her plate. All eyes turned to her. "My husband is dead. If anyone has reason to mourn, it is I. Now, let us enjoy our food in peace."

Vicky took a bite of her eggs. Never had she tasted anything so perfectly cooked. As a matter of fact, everything she had put on her plate was delectable. She took another bite, and when she looked up, she found the duchess staring at her. What Vicky had eaten thus far turned in her stomach. Was she eating too quickly? Had she done something offensive in the way she cut her food? God forbid if she upset a new widow!

Setting her fork aside, Vicky took a drink of her hot chocolate in hopes the woman would stop staring. It was not until the duchess returned her attention to her own food that Vicky allowed herself to breathe again.

As they continued to eat, Lord Gerard asked about the gentleman's fishing expedition. Soon, the men were discussing all they would do that day. As each man spoke, Vicky found her mind returning to the duke's death. Who had poisoned him? And why?

Yet, these were not the only questions that had her mind churning, for Richard and the duchess exchanged several more smiles during the course of the meal. Was it possible the two were lovers and had conspired to kill the duke? The day before, she would have considered such a notion absurd, but given their reaction to the duke's death as well as the present conversation, nothing was out of the realm of possibility.

"Let us hope the constable allows us to enjoy the day," Richard said. "Although the death of the duke is tragic, we cannot allow it to hinder the outings he had planned for us."

The duchess set her glass on the table. "The constable mentioned that my husband wrote but one word, "betrayed," on a piece of parchment. This has now caused us to look upon one another with suspicion." She lifted a finger and a footman hurried to her side. "Bring in the constable at once."

Vicky stared around the table. Who had the duchess meant when she mentioned looks of suspicion? If an outsider entered the room at that moment, he would never have known there had been a murder the night before!

"Charlotte, what are you doing?" Lady Warwick asked. "The duke would fall over dead if he knew a constable was in his dining room."

"The duke is already dead," the duchess rebutted. "And I have an idea who may have killed him."

Constable Cogwell entered the room. "Your Grace," he said with a deep bow, "I am here to serve you in order to see that His Grace's soul may be at peace."

Lord Warwick gave a sad shake of his head, and his wife scolded him with her eyes. The baron leaned back in his chair as if preparing for escape. Yet, it was Richard who Vicky found the most curious of them all, for he was grinning!

"From footman to stable hand," the duchess said, "we employ dozens of people. My husband has given us a clue as to how this terrible crime was committed but not by whom."

"Forgive me, Your Grace," the constable said. "I do not understand."

"Is it not obvious?" the duchess asked. "Our guests are clearly innocent, as is my husband's family. Therefore, it must be one of the staff who poisoned my husband. Perhaps it was because he could not name his murderer. What man of privilege, even if he is a duke, knows the names of all his servants?"

Vicky recalled a time during her youth when her cousin had been caught stealing a sweet. The boy had tried to cast blame on someone other than himself by giving a story about a highwayman who sneaked into the house. It had not taken her uncle long to pull the truth from his son who finally admitted he had been the thief. The duchess was doing something very similar.

It was not that Vicky believed the duchess guilty, but to cast blame on one of the servants in order to draw attention away from those much more likely to have committed the crime was absurd. What was worse was the constable grinned as if he were a child receiving a pinch on the cheek. Surely the man was above such foolishness!

"Excellent wisdom, indeed!" Constable Cogwell said. Clearly he was not above the foolishness, after all. "I am honored to receive such guidance from a lady of your stature. May I be so bold as to make a request? Since the inquest will take more time than I had initially believed, may I be provided a guest room? I may be here for several days."

The duchess thought for a moment and then replied, "The guest house at the far side of the gardens will be made ready for your use. Thank you, Constable. You may leave us."

The constable hurried from the room. The guests grinned from ear to ear, and why would they not? One was a murderer, and the duchess had sent the very man who was to investigate the murder off on a fox hunt with no fox to be found.

"Now that we have cleared that up and the constable knows in which direction to go," Lord Warwick said, "let us plan our excursion. I have the most pleasant morning planned. In fact—"

"Miss Parker," the duchess said, speaking over her stepson, "you are to join me in the sitting room in an hour." It was not a request, it was a command. And one did not deny a duchess anything she wished.

"I would be honored," Vicky replied.

"My head is aching," Lady Warwick said. "I am going to rest."

The duchess replied with a roll of her eyes as she stood. The others followed suit. Then, to Vicky's shock, the duchess winked at Richard!

When all but James and Vicky had gone, following the duchess from the room like chicks following their mother, James hurried to Vicky. "Did you really speak with Richard Kent last night?" he asked. "It is none of my business what you were doing, but I am curious as to why you would spend any amount of time with the man."

Vicky went to reply, but a footman entered the room. It was not safe to continue the conversation where anyone could overhear, even the servants. "Why yes," she replied with a forced smile, "I would love to take a stroll with you through the gardens."

***

Morning dew clung stubbornly to blades of grass as James and Vicky walked down the cobbled path through the expansive garden. Once they were some distance from the house, Vicky glanced over her shoulder and came to a stop.

"Have you ever seen such madness?" she asked. "The duke has been murdered and everyone is acting as if it is a hindrance to their day rather than the tragedy it is."

"I cannot say that I have," James replied. "Tell me, what happened last night after I went to my room?"

Vicky explained how she had entered the duke's study and what she had seen. Of course, she left out the part about forgetting to curtsy and not realizing the man was dead until minutes later.

"It is odd that Richard Kent created an alibi for me. I honestly believe he did it only to save his own hide and not mine." She said the last with a firm nod, her conviction was that strong.

"What you say is plausible, but if the duke owed the man money, why kill him?" He paused and raised a brow. "Unless he had already been paid. It is not as if he would reveal such information to you."

"I had not considered that," Vicky said. "Maybe the debt was late, and Richard killed him out of spite. Or perhaps it was because he has eyes for the duchess. Did you notice how they looked at one another all morning?"

"I did!" James replied. "For I, too, have that look at times…" He looked down. "That is…I mean…"

Vicky grinned. "Do tell!" she insisted, pleased her friend had found a woman to whom he could show his affection. "Is it Laura?" She clasped her hands in joy. "It is her, is it not?"

"Yes," James replied, but his response lacked enthusiasm. "Now, regarding the duchess and Mr. Kent. I saw what you saw. They are sharing in some sort of secret, that much is certain."

"I've never even been inside the great 'ouse, sir!" a frantic voice said, causing Vicky and James to start. "I'll swear on the 'oly Bible, I will!"

"Then tell me who has, or I shall see you hanged!" That was the voice of the constable.

"I-I wouldn't know, sir," the other voice said. "A-ask the stable hand! Yes, maybe it were him, but it sure weren't me!"

Vicky shook her head. "We cannot allow an innocent person to take the blame for what transpired. It is inhumane. I could investigate far better than that man!"

James stared at her in shock. "Are you saying you wish to do your own inquest into finding the murderer?"

That was exactly what Vicky planned to do. She could easily enjoy the day just as the others were and simply go on with her life. However, the duke had been kind in inviting her, and knowing his life was cut short by the hand of another stirred a bit of anger inside her. She did not grieve his loss, for she barely knew him, but he deserved better treatment. Plus, too many men who walked this earth had gotten away with crimes and other forms of cruelty. Perhaps by finding the true killer, it would balance the scales of justice – as slight as it might be.

As she considered these things, she looked up at James, who smiled at her as he often did. She never understood why the man had never married. Instead he had chosen to live a solitary life. He was handsome, intelligent, and a dear friend. Maybe it was his missing fingers that caused him to withdraw from others, but he was as much a man as any.

"Yes, I will find the killer as a gift to the duke," she replied. "For my conscience will not allow me to look the other way. However, I cannot do it alone. I will need your help."

When her father had died, she had made the same request of James then as she did now, but it had been concerning the business. Not only had he readily agreed, but he had remained patient as he guided her through the aspects of accounting that went beyond the simple tasks her father had taught her.

And just like that time, James replied, "Of course I will. For what is a friend who does not help another in a time of need?"

They discussed their plan. James would gather information from the men during their fishing expedition, and Vicky would do the same with the women. Including the duchess, who Vicky learned had not given a response to her whereabouts the previous night.

After wishing each other good luck, James returned to the house and Vicky continued her stroll through the gardens alone. Stopping at a bed of red and blue forget-me-nots, she stared at them as her mind wandered.

She had seen flowers like these before, although they were not in a garden but rather grew wild in a field. Vicky rested on a soft blanket, a picnic basket and a bottle of wine beside her. The man for whom she cared deeply sat beside her and offered her a blue flower. The simple gesture had warmed her heart as the first pangs of what she thought were love came over her.

"Would you prefer blue or red?"

Vicky started and turned to find Richard Kent standing behind her. "Neither if it is you who makes the offer," she replied. "Are you not joining the other men?"

"I am," Richard replied. "But I wished to speak to you first. You were quiet at breakfast, which I found unusual."

"Unusual?" she asked. "How would you know what is my usual amount of discourse? Do you wish to hear how I will spend my day? I believe it will begin with several hours of embroidery."

Richard raised his eyebrows. "Typically when one is quiet, she is gathering information by listening."

"And when one is talkative," Victoria retorted, "it is because he is attempting to distract. Is there something you wish to confess?"

"There is," he said. "I confess that I do not trust you. I fear you may plant seeds of doubt in the others to place blame on me." Vicky went to respond, but her breath caught in her throat when he took a menacing step forward. "You would not do such a thing, would you?"

"If you are asking if I am like you," she retorted, "I am not. In fact—"

Richard grasped her hand and raised it to his lips, cutting her words short. "I knew you would never betray me, not after seeing your eyes on me during breakfast. It is bold for a woman to give a man such looks, but rest assured I do not judge you. I admit that I welcome your gaze."

Pulling her hand away, Vicky scowled. "I can assure you, Mr. Kent, that whatever looks I may have given you had nothing to do with romance but rather of suspicion."

"All women are the same," he said, sighing. "They deny what they feel for me, but what can I do about it? For now, I must join the others, but rest assured, we will speak later." He turned and began to walk away. "Remember, Vicky, do not betray me," he called over his shoulder. "I saved you from the gallows!"

"You saved yourself," she replied in frustration. "Also, only my closest friends call me Vicky, and you, Mr. Kent, are no friend!"

Chapter Six

Upon entering the sitting room, Vicky found the duchess gazing out the window.

"Please close the door behind you," the woman said without turning to face Vicky.

The door clicked closed and Vicky stood waiting, unsure what to do next. She had not been offered a chair, and one simply did not sit without an outright invitation. Especially in the presence of a duchess. Not that it mattered. If she was to remain standing where she was, so be it.

"My husband spoke highly of your bookkeeping abilities," the duchess said. "I understand the enterprise belonged to your father, who passed away some time ago, is that correct?"

"Indeed, Your Grace," Vicky replied. "Fortunately, his assistant, Mr. Kensington, remained and has continued the good work my father began many years ago." She clasped her hands in front of her and bowed her head. "My condolences for the loss of your husband."

"The duke was a good man," the duchess replied. "Oftentimes stingy with his money but still a worthy husband." She turned and the sun glinted on her blond curls. Vicky suspected that the black mourning dress she wore cost more than a year's wages for most. "We have been married just under two years," the duchess continued. "And although his death is shocking, I am afraid it is not unexpected."

Vicky could not hide her surprise. "Oh? Was His Grace in poor health?" If Vicky could have described the older man, the description would not have included sickly, even at his advanced age.

"He was past his seventieth year," the duchess said as she walked over to a wingback chair. "I am but twenty." She shrugged. "It was only a matter of time before he died." Once she was seated and her skirts in place, she motioned to the matching chair across from her. "Please, sit."

"Thank you, Your Grace," Vicky said, doing as the woman bade. As she smoothed the skirts of her own dress, she considered how to move the conversation further along without causing offense. It would not be easy, for she had one particular path she hoped to take. "It appears Mr. Kent is grief-stricken. Were he and the duke close?"

The duchess laughed, a light, airy sound. It was no wonder the duke had married this woman, for she had an air of grace about her. "Close?" she asked, still chuckling. "Not at all. They could not stand being in the presence of one another, yet they often were."

The door opened, and the butler entered with a silver tray. Once he had served the tea, he bowed his way out of the room.

"As I was saying, Felton and Richard were not close, but they spent a great deal of time playing games of chance together. That was the only reason Richard was allowed in our home. Personally, I believe the man is a charlatan."

At least we agree on one point, Vicky thought.

"Felton did not think twice at losing a thousand pounds in baccarat, nor ten times that amount to leave for India. However, whenever I requested a new dress, I was forced to listen to him rant for an hour about the responsibility those of our station have when it comes to money. Last night, he was more concerned with his little meetings than to hear of my heart's wishes." Her cheeks turned pink. "It is why I fell asleep in the library with a glass of wine in my hand, just as I have many times before." She sighed. "It is unlike me to speak so openly about my troubles, but there it is."

It did not take a scholar to see that the marriage had been rife with tension. It was quite obvious the duke's second wife was under duress. If she was to be believed.

"I admit," Vicky said, "when His Grace announced his plans to relocate to India, I was surprised. I imagine you were pleased."

The duchess set her teacup on its saucer with an angry *clink*. "Pleased?" she asked with affront. "I was irate! It is why we argued in the library after his grand announcement, which was not all that uncommon. I may have no say in any decision my husband made, but I wanted my voice to be heard about this matter!" Her voice had risen, and her face reddened to her ears. She lowered her voice once more. "As the wife of a duke, my only duty is to look beautiful and be obedient. I have no doubt I meet the former without argument, so much so he often became jealous."

"You are beautiful," Vicky said, uncertain if the woman was looking for validation but affirming her point would gain her favor. "And yes, men tend to be jealous creatures."

"That they are," the duchess replied with a smile. "And quite often it is for unfounded reasons. Then again, there are times when their jealousy is justified. A woman's awareness of these truths gives her some voice in her home."

Vicky hid her smile behind her teacup. Was the duchess alluding to a possible relationship with Richard Kent?

"And you Miss Parker? May I ask if you were intending to make Mr. Kensington jealous at breakfast this morning?"

Vicky choked on her tea. "I beg your pardon?" she said. "I have no reason to make him jealous. We are nothing more than partners in the business and nothing more."

"Is that so?" the duchess replied with something akin to amusement. "I thought your smiles for Mr. Kent were meant to stir envy in Mr. Kensington. My mistake." Her mischievous grin said she believed no mistake had been made.

"And what is your opinion of Mr. Kent?" Vicky asked.

The duchess gave a derisive sniff. "I find the man barely tolerable if you must know."

Pushing aside her annoyance and seizing the opportunity, Vicky said, "I noticed an exchange of smiles between the two of you and thought it some custom of which I was unaware. That was why I chose to participate. One does not enjoy being excluded, do they? Or was I mistaken with what I saw?"

The corners of the duchess's lips twitched. "Indeed, we did smile at one another, but not for reasons you may believe. One of us expressed victory and the other defeat. Can you guess which was mine?"

The woman's gaze was so piercing, Vicky's cup shook in her hand as she set it on its saucer. It had been her intention to make inquiries of the duchess, and now she had become the object of an inquest herself. How quickly the tables had turned.

"Answer carefully, Miss Parker, for your response will tell me whether or not you are responsible for the death of my husband."

While the glare the duchess had fixed upon Vicky had conjured fear, the woman's words now brought about a sense of panic. "May I ask a question before I respond?"

"I see no harm in that," the duchess replied.

"You stated you do not like Mr. Kent," Vicky said, choosing her words carefully. "However, since His Grace gamed with the man, he was here often. Am I correct thus far?"

"You are."

"Then I believe the smile you gave him was one of victory, for now that the duke is gone, Mr. Kent will no longer have a reason to call."

The room fell silent, and Vicky braced herself for an outburst that would lead to her being thrown out of the house. Or worse, have the constable sent for so she could be arrested.

"You are correct," the duchess replied with a pleased look. "Now I know for certain you did not murder my husband."

The air returned to Vicky's lungs. She did not understand the woman's reasoning, but as long as no fingers were pointed at her, she was relieved.

"Thank you for believing me, Your Grace," Vicky said. "Who do you believe is the culprit, then?"

"I have no doubt one of the guests committed the murder," the duchess continued, "but it was not you."

Confusion washed over Vicky. "Forgive me, but did you not say you believed it was a servant?"

The duchess laughed. "That was only a distraction to put the real killer at ease and to keep that foolish constable occupied for the remainder of the day." She held out her hand and studied the large ruby on a gold band on her finger. "The killer of my dear Felton must have something to gain from his death. Of course, it would not be anything as trivial as jewelry. I have plenty, so therefore it cannot be me."

"So you believe the duke was murdered because of greed?"

The duchess said as she rose from her chair. "Of course that was the reason," she replied. "And George stands to gain the most now that my husband is dead. He never approved of his father's marriage to me, for I am young and beautiful. With his father out of the way, he will now be able to take over the dukedom and force me to live on a pittance. I will likely end up in a tiny cottage with an allowance that will not provide me enough to buy the new dresses I so need. That is not the life a dowager duchess should be forced to live!"

Vicky could think of a thousand worse ways to spend one's life, but she kept those thoughts to herself. "You make a good point," she said aloud, "but Lord Warwick, like you, was asleep at the time of the murder. If he sneaked out of his room, surely he would have woken his wife."

The duchess snorted. "Lavinia snores so loudly that an elephant on her bed would not wake her." She shook her head. "No, I have no doubt it was George, for he has the most to gain."

"Your Grace," Vicky said, "with all due respect, why have you not shared your concerns with Constable Cogwell? Surely your word—"

"Prevails over that of a soon-to-be duke?" the duchess asked with a sniff. "I may be a duchess, but I am still a woman. If I did speak my mind, George would surely throw me out into the streets with nothing."

Vicky tried to imagine the soft-spoken Lord Warwick committing murder – or throwing a woman, any woman, into the streets – and could not. Yet, there was a motive there.

"If you hear anything or find proof that George committed this horrible crime, do let me know," the duchess said. "I trust no one else, so please keep this conversation between us. And as for the constable, I will see he is kept out of your way."

Vicky was uncertain from where this sudden trust came, but she would use it to her advantage. "Do I have your permission to look wherever necessary to see what evidence I am able to gather?"

The duchess smiled. "Treat my house as your own," she said. "Do whatever you must to find George guilty of murdering his father."

***

With permission to explore the house as her own, Vicky did just that, returning first to the scene of the crime. The study was easier to see in daylight. And without a dead body sitting in the chair behind the desk.

Ornate bookshelves of dark oak housed numerous tomes. The desk looked just as it had the night before, minus the dead body of the duke. The decanter and two glasses still sat on the desk and, to Vicky's surprise, so was the parchment with the word 'betrayed' scrawled on it.

She picked up the paper and turned it over, disappointed not to find a name written there. Returning the scrap to the desk, she turned her attention to the glasses – one empty and one full.

Whoever poisoned the duke must have sat with him and made a reasonable excuse to refuse the drink. Yet how did the poison get into the brandy without his knowledge? Or had it been added only to the duke's glass and the full glass contained no poison? She was not about ready to sip the second glass to find out!

Her eyes fell on a small cart in the corner with several decanters and clean glasses. She approached it and looked over the contents. She sighed when she found nothing of importance. It was silly to expect to find a sachet of poison or a trinket that would give away who the killer was, anyway.

"Think!" she whispered, tapping a finger on her forehead.

She imagined herself as the murderer, and for some reason it was a cloaked figure in her mind's eye. "May I pour you a drink, Your Grace?" she said in imitation of the killer.

"That is awfully kind of you," she responded in a gruff voice in an attempt to sound like the duke.

She then pretended to pour a measure into the empty glass. The person then likely took the seat across from the duke.

Vicky sat in the chair behind the desk. "Why not have some for yourself," she said in the duke's voice as she lifted the empty glass.

She hurried to the opposite chair. "Why, thank you, Your Grace," she responded for the murderer.

"He then poured a measure for himself," Vicky mused, pretending to pour into the full glass. She frowned. "But he did not drink. Why?" Then she snapped her fingers. "That's it!" she said. "The poison was already in the bottle!"

Vicky reached for the decanter, removed the stopper, and dared to take a small sniff. The aroma of rich brandy greeted her but there was no putrid smell she guessed poison might smell like. Then again, she had no idea what odor poison had. Nevertheless, the murderer must have poisoned the bottle beforehand.

Making a mental note, she returned the stopper and replaced the decanter before continuing her perusal of the desktop. A ledger lay to one side, and she flipped through the pages. The first two contained nothing more than a summary of his accounting, which she and James had completed for him. When she turned the page, however, she found a loose piece of parchment. On it was a list of names and times.

Gerard: Half past ten
Lavinia: Quarter to eleven
George: Eleven O'clock
Kent: Eleven fifteen
Charlotte: Half-past eleven
Miss Parker: Midnight

So, Richard had lied about the hour of his appointment, which was forty-five minutes earlier than Vicky's. Why had he shown up during her appointed time?

Furthermore, there were no notes that explained the topics that were to be discussed at each meeting, but Vicky intended to find out what they were. She refolded the paper and slid it into the pocket of her dress.

"What are you doing here?"

Vicky's heart jumped into her throat as she spun around to find Lady Warwick marching into the room, her green gown swooshing around her ankles. "Speak now before I summon the constable!"

Vicky remembered that the duchess had asked her not to reveal that she was investigating, so she replied, "The ledger. It is the summary of the duke's holdings, which I, or rather my father's firm completed for him. I wanted to ascertain that there were no other services which would need our attention."

Lady Warwick glanced at the ledger and then looked at Vicky. She brushed a strand of dark hair from her face and sighed. "Forgive me for raising my voice," she said. "The death of the duke has affected us all greatly and I am concerned about my husband. George is unable to handle most situations well, but the death of his father is all the more difficult. I fear this is weighing heavy on him."

Although Vicky had never been married, she could feel the heaviness of the woman's burdens. Of course she was frustrated. Her father-in-law had been murdered and her husband insisted everyone remain and enjoy the weekend. It was most definitely a strange reaction to such a horrible event.

"I understand, my lady," Vicky said. "There is no need to apologize to me." In all honesty, she was surprised at the woman's acknowledgment, for no marchioness, and soon-to-be duchess, ever had reason to apologize to anyone, especially a woman so far below her station.

"You are as graceful in your mercy as you are beautiful," Lady Warwick said, taking Vicky by the hand. "Come. Let us go join Charlotte so we may hear all about her woes in life." Vicky could not help but smile when the woman winked at her.

They made their way to the sitting room, where the duchess was speaking to her lady's maid.

"I must begin my time of mourning," she was saying. "You must go at once and instruct every dressmaker in the area that they open their shops to me and no one else beginning Tuesday afternoon. I will need an entirely new wardrobe appropriate for the occasion."

The maid curtsied. "Yes, Your Grace. I will go at once." She then hurried from the room.

The duchess let out a long sigh. "Mourning will bring attention to me, and I will not embarrass Felton by wearing these old rags."

Lady Warwick sat on a lounge, but Vicky remained standing.

"Do be polite to our guest, Charlotte," the marchioness said. "The poor woman stands as a servant waiting for permission to sit."

The duchess's eyes widened and she turned toward Vicky. "Why, Victoria and I are great friends, are we not? In fact, I asked her earlier never to wait on my account."

Although the woman had said no such thing, Vicky nodded her agreement and took a seat on the couch. The glare that passed between the other two women did not escape her attention.

"I imagine the men are enjoying their outing," Vicky said.

"George does find solace in fishing," Lady Warwick replied. "His father refused to accompany him. He was far too busy pursuing simpler things in life." She smiled at the duchess as she said this.

"My husband spent the majority of his time working," the duchess retorted. "Securing the hearty estate his fool of a son and greedy daughter-in-law will likely bring to ruin once they have gotten their claws into it. I am here alone in despair while his flesh and blood goes out to muddy the very shoes he wore with such dignity."

Lady Warwick sniffed. "George is entertaining his guests, not sending servants out to schedule the making of new dresses."

The duchess frowned. "I do it to honor my husband." She glanced around the room. "In fact, I will call in someone next month to discuss changing the décor in several of these rooms. No expense will be spared in bringing the house to the level of luxury Felton wanted."

"You mean to spend his money before my George takes control of it," Lady Warwick snapped. She removed a handkerchief from her sleeve and dabbed at her nose. "It is clear you think only of yourself."

"You are merely jealous of my beauty," the duchess replied.

As the two traded insults, Vicky recalled the many times in life she had felt awkward. Anticipating her first kiss among the flowers of a field was in the forefront. Also on the list was the encounter with a distant cousin of her father who dropped most of his consonants when he spoke. He became irate when Vicky could not understand him. Now the argument between these two women could be added to that list. If it were her place, she would have intervened, but it was not.

"Let us ask Miss Parker her opinion," the duchess said, much to Vicky's horror. "What say you?"

Vicky swallowed hard. She had stopped listening long ago. "Your Grace?"

"Who is more at fault in her disrespect to the duke's passing? Is it I for wanting to honor his memory by selecting a new dress and bringing this estate to life? Or is it his son, who chooses to go play in a lake like a child?"

Two sets of eyes stared at her, and Vicky wished she could run away. Far away. Yet, she recalled the wisdom her father had given her: *There was always middle ground*, he was wont to say. *Seek that, and you will find peace in any situation.*

"Everyone grieves in his or her own way," Vicky replied. "Therefore, neither can be wrong. As long as the memory of the duke is honored, that is what is important."

For a moment, the only sound Vicky could hear was her own heartbeat in her ears. Would the duchess do as she threatened and send the constable after her? Or would the marchioness see her thrown out of the house?

"There is a new millinery located near Fleet," Lady Warwick said. "I believe you will find their options the best in all of London. They will be wonderful accessories for your new dresses."

"That is kind of you, Lavinia," the duchess said. "Perhaps I can ask your advice on the new décor?"

Vicky stared. How could two ladies drop all propriety and argue like children one minute and resume dignity and discuss fashion the next as if they had not had any disagreement?

As the butler placed a tray with tea and cakes on the coffee table, Vicky remained quiet, hoping her opinion would keep the two from clawing out each other's eyes before the weekend came to an end and Vicky could make her escape back to common sense.

Chapter Seven

No sooner had the door closed behind the duchess after she excused herself for "some time alone to mourn" than Lady Warwick leaped from her seat, her hands clenched at her side.

"Time to mourn?" she growled. "In all my life, I have never met anyone who could lie so well. The woman is happy the duke's dead." She turned to Vicky. "Do you know why they argued so often?"

Vicky took the last sip of her tea as she tried to decide how to respond. To gossip about a duchess was in poor taste, but it was worse when it was done in her own home. "Argued?" she asked as if surprised. "But they appeared to be the happiest of couples."

Lady Warwick shook her head. "Oh, my poor child. How easily you are fooled." She walked over to stare out the window. "I cannot blame you, however. The duke did everything possible to make his life appear normal, but I can assure you, it was not."

Vicky rose from her chair. "What do you mean?"

"At eleven o'clock last night, I met with George's father. He complained that the joy of the anticipation of his travels to India was dampened by Charlotte's refusal to accompany him."

Vicky joined the marchioness at the window. "I was under the impression she shared his excitement of going to India."

"That is what she wanted everyone to believe," Lady Warwick replied with a snort. "Trust me, she wanted nothing less. The duke confided as much to me. Of course, she had no say in whether she went or remained, unless…" She turned to Vicky. "Unless the duke suddenly perished."

Vicky had never been one for believing in signs, but as soon as the words left the woman's mouth, thick storm clouds covered the sun, drenching the marchioness in shadow. Could it be that the duchess herself killed her husband so she would not be forced to relocate?

"Did you happen to share in a drink with His Grace during your meeting last night?" Vicky asked.

"A drink?" Lady Warwick asked with a frown. "No, he would never go so far as to offer a drink to a woman during a scheduled meeting. We spoke of the duties George would take on once the duke was gone." She sighed. "Which meant that everything would remain the same. One would think His Grace would have given my husband more responsibilities to ready him for the day he takes over the dukedom, but he refused at every turn. Yet, I suppose that point is moot now that my husband will become the new duke in reality."

"Lord Warwick is fortunate that you are here to support him as you do," Vicky said in an attempt to gain the marchioness's favor, thus hoping to garner more information. Not that the woman was not already candid enough with her family's troubles. "Not many women possess your abilities."

The words seemed to make their mark, for Lady Lavinia nodded in agreement. "I am glad you recognize that which many do not. It is I who makes all the preparations for everything in this estate as well as the one in London. While George spends his days napping and the duke pursues his business interests, I manage the rest. I oversee their schedules, remind them of upcoming meetings, write letters for them. One would believe I am an assistant here rather than George's wife."

"And what of the duchess?" Vicky asked with an air of concern. "Surely she does her part to help."

The marchioness snorted. "That little chit of a girl?" she asked and then glanced around. Perhaps she was expecting the duchess to appear out of thin air and chastise her. Vicky would have had that worry if it were she who said something so impertinent about a duchess. Lady Warwick lowered her voice. "Charlotte is barely off leading strings and lacks any form of proper training. How could she possibly help?"

Vicky considered all the woman had told her. It appeared few were happy with the duke, least of all the marchioness. Nor did anyone approve of his marriage to the duchess. The problem now was that Vicky had yet to learn the whereabouts of this woman when the duke had been murdered.

"When I went to meet with the duke," Vicky said, "or rather when Mr. Kent and I went to speak to him and we found him dead, there were two glasses on his desk. One contained a full measure of brandy and the other was empty. Were they there when you had your meeting by chance?"

"Miss Parker," Lady Warwick replied, her eyes narrowing, "before I answer, I have a question of my own. Why are you lying to me?"

"Excuse me?" Vicky asked, taken aback. "I tell no lies. I did find the decanter of brandy and two glasses on the duke's desk alongside the note."

Lady Warwick clicked her tongue. "I speak not of that nor the message written in haste. What I want to know is why you insist on lying that you entered the study in the company of Mr. Kent. Are you protecting him for some reason?"

Vicky's mouth went dry. *She knows!* But how?

There was no sense in lying any longer. "The truth is Mr. Kent entered the room moments after I did. He offered to claim we were together so the blame would not be passed to me."

The marchioness smiled as she took Vicky by the hand. "The man cares for no one but himself," she said. "You must know that this act of chivalry is for his benefit and nothing more."

"Oh, I have no doubt that is true," Vicky replied. "But I can assure you, I did not harm the duke in any way."

Lady Warwick ignored her plea. "My meeting with the duke ran no more than ten minutes, and as I was returning to my room, I came upon Mr. Kent, who was spying in the hallway."

"Spying? On whom?"

"Our beloved widow," Lady Warwick replied. "She was in the library with Lord Gerard. Oh, do not look so shocked, my dear. Charlotte has had numerous affairs. The baron is simply her most recent. That is the reason His Grace no longer wished to do business with the man."

The sun emerged from behind the clouds and sent rays cascading through the window once more. If what the marchioness said was true concerning the duchess and Lord Gerard, it gave Her Grace a strong motive for murdering her husband. Love could make people do the strangest things.

Vicky still was not convinced, however. "Lord Warwick stands to gain much from the death of the duke," she said. "Why would the duchess kill him when she stands to gain nothing?"

"Nothing?" Lady Warwick said with a laugh. "She is to inherit this estate and will receive an allowance that would make any lady drool with envy. But this has nothing to do with money. No, the death of the duke was about freedom. Freedom from the confines of matrimony and freedom from relocation to India. Charlotte will now be able to partake in her dubious ways without any threats lingering over her."

"You said that you saw Mr. Kent in the hallway," Vicky said. "What happened when he saw you? Did you speak to him?"

Lady Warwick shook her head. "The snake hurried past me in the direction of the duke's study without so much as a word of greeting. Once he was gone, I pressed my ear to the door of the library to see upon whom he was eavesdropping." She leaned forward and lowered her voice. "I overheard Charlotte and Lord Gerard speaking."

"Did you?" Vicky asked, gasping as she had heard many ladies do when they wanted to engage in gossip without seeming to. "And what did they say?"

With an air of conspiracy about her, the marchioness leaned in closer. "They were speaking of their future together. Lord Gerard's exact words were, 'With the duke now out of the way, we can be together.'"

Vicky could only stare at the woman in shock. "He did not!"

"He did," Lady Warwick said with a firm nod. "I would not have believed it myself if I had not heard it with my own ears."

"What happened next?" Vicky asked.

"I heard someone else approach," Lady Warwick replied. "I did not wait to see who it was. My head was aching, so I went to the kitchen for a headache powder and then returned to my room to find my husband snoring away as he always is."

The marchioness returned to her chair, but Vicky remained at the window. The woman had made mention of an aching head in the morning. Had the powder not helped?

That did not matter, however, for other more important questions swirled in her mind. Could it be that the duchess had poisoned the brandy and asked Lord Gerard to deliver it? If so, was the baron merely a pawn who knew nothing about the scheme, or had he been a willing participant?

Then there was the issue of every person insisting he or she was asleep in their rooms when it was evident that they had not been.

Indeed, Mr. Kent was standing outside the library door listening, the baron and the duchess were behind that very door, and Lady Warwick was in the corridor. The only person she had no true answer for his whereabouts was the marquess. Perhaps he was the only one who had not lied about being abed at the time.

Vicky now had more questions than answers!

"May I ask why you did not inform the constable of what you overheard?" Vicky asked. "Surely he would focus his inquest on them."

"If I were to do that, I would have to inform my husband, and he certainly would not wish to offend a guest. But even if I did, it would appear as if I were trying to implicate Charlotte for my own gain. No, the truth will reveal itself soon enough, and Charlotte will be held accountable for her crimes. And the baron, as well, of course.

The man knew what he was doing. He was angry that the duke revealed in front of everyone that he was revoking his investments. That kind of humiliation will sour anyone's disposition."

Vicky recalled that the baron had indeed looked none too pleased last evening with the duke's announcement. And it was becoming clearer that the duchess herself had much more to gain than she had admitted.

***

Having excused herself to take in fresh air, Vicky wandered toward the large stables, where the constable was speaking to one of the hands. The craftsmanship of the building was of better quality than even that in which sat the accounting office, and this was merely a stable. The white paint was so bright it appeared to have been applied that morning, and the area that surrounded it was swept clean of hay or other evidence that horses were stabled inside.

Just outside the main doors, Constable Cogwell argued with a man Vicky did not recognize.

She approached them, pausing in the shadow of a nearby tree to listen to the conversation.

"I'm tellin' ya," the stable hand said. "I ain't been inside that 'ouse 'cept for when His Grace 'ired me for this position. That was ten years this past winter! An' why would 'is Grace wanna share a drink with the likes of me? Next thing ya know, you'll wonder if the King's me cousin." He crossed his arms over his chest and leaned against the stable wall. "You're gonna blame this on me, ain't ya? Well, you won't take me in without a fight, I tell ya. Mark me words on that!"

"You will hold your tongue with me, Corter," Constable Cogwell snapped. "I have the power to do what I must. Now, if you did not commit the murder, who did? Hurry now. Give me a name before I summon the Bow Street Runners to collect you."

Vicky shook her head. What would the Bow Street Runners be doing this far outside of London? Then again, how would this man know they limited their duties to the city?

Upon hearing the name of the infamous and powerful enforcers, the stable hand's stern look faded, replaced by horror. "It must've been one of the maids in the great 'ouse!" he cried. "Give it a think. They're all pretty and could've sneaked into 'is Grace's room with nothin' more'n a smile and then killed 'im!"

"Why would a maid poison the duke?" the constable demanded.

Corter placed a hand on his heart. "'Cause women're spiteful, sir. Me Mary never forgave me for what she calls 'infractions' I did fifteen years ago! I made mention of her cousin bein' pretty, and she's never forgivin' me." He leaned forward and lowered his voice. "Sometimes I wonder if she'll poison me stew one night."

To Vicky's disbelief, the constable made a notation in his notebook. Was he considering asking this man's wife if she had poisoned the duke based on nothing more than a flippant statement made by her husband?

"Miss Parker," Constable Cogwell said when he noticed her standing nearby, "are you enjoying this fine day?"

"I am," Vicky replied. "May I ask how your inquest is going?"

The man produced a handkerchief and wiped sweat from his brow, the bushy eyebrows sticking straight up. "Murder is not an appropriate subject for conversation with a lady, but as you are not a lady, I see no reason I cannot discuss my findings with you."

Vicky schooled her features to contain her indignation. She may not be a lady in the sense of the nobility, but that did not make her less of a woman deserving of respect.

No, wait, this was a good thing! If the constable saw her as one in whom he could confide, she would know everything he knew.

The constable glanced at the tiny scratches he had made on his pad. "I believe someone with access to the great house, as well as the duke's office, committed this terrible crime."

"How observant," Vicky muttered dryly before realizing she had said the words aloud. She gave him her best smile and waved a hand as if cooling her face. "I do hope you find the murderer soon. It is so frightening that someone willing to take the life of another roams this estate a free person."

"You have nothing to fear," Constable Cogwell replied with the condescension of most men. "After a bite to eat, I will nap and then continue my inquest. I predict I will have the killer in custody before sunset."

He moved to walk past her, but Vicky called his attention once more. "Constable, have you considered the decanter of brandy?" she asked as if it had just occurred to her. "How did the duke come to possess it do you think?"

"Now, Miss Parker, I must insist that you not ask such silly questions," he replied with a chuckle. "It was purchased from a shop, of course. Where else would he have gotten it?"

Vicky had to press her lips together to keep herself from the retort that settled in her throat.

"The guilt of this crime resides in but one person," the constable continued. "By interviewing everyone, it will put pressure on the guilty party to come forward." He shook his head as he walked past her, mumbling the word "decanter" followed by a laugh.

"Very well," Vicky whispered as she watched Constable Cogwell disappear. "If you are unwilling to take any suggestions, you leave me no choice. I will find the murderer myself."

Resuming her stroll, Vicky worked through what she had learned thus far, which was clearly more than the constable seemed to know.

She was uncertain how long she had been in deep thought when someone spoke her name, making her start. She turned, her hand to her breast so her heart would not burst from her chest, as James approached.

"You startled me!"

"I am sorry," he said with a smile. "We returned from the fishing expedition only moments ago, so I came in search of you." His smile widened. "And I am glad I found you. Did you learn anything of importance this morning?"

"More than I would have expected," she replied. "For one, no one was in his or her room when they said they were. Come, let us walk and I will explain everything."

James held out an arm and Vicky stared at it. Although she thought it a kind gesture, she felt a sense of trepidation. The last time she allowed a man to walk with her thus had ended in heartbreak.

"Sorry," James said, dropping his arm. "I was just taking what I have learned from the gentlemen here and offering as they would have. I meant nothing by it."

She shook the memories from her head. James was her friend. "No, it is all right." She placed a hand on his arm. "Now, let me tell you what I gathered from the two women who seem to be at war with one another."

As they walked together, she explained what she had learned and the frustration of not knowing whether there was any truth to either of their stories. She then moved to her conversation with the constable, and when she finished, she heaved a heavy sigh. Speaking aloud what she knew made her reconsider her previous insistence to solve the case.

"So, you see, I learned a bit more, yet I feel no closer to the truth than I did before. Perhaps I should give up and allow the constable to do his job."

James came to an abrupt halt. "You cannot do that!" he said. "You are the most intelligent person here. Plus, you have never been a woman who accepts defeat."

Vicky's heart fluttered as he looked down at her, and she dropped her gaze only to find that her hand was still on his arm. She quickly pulled it away. "You are kind to say so," she managed to say through a throat so arid they could have been in the Sahara Desert. She had to change the subject, and soon! "And what did you learn while fishing?"

James flicked his fingers in the water of a nearby birdbath. "Well, first of all, Lord Warwick is a decent man, yet he allows everyone to treat him as if he is nothing but an annoyance. Lord Gerard demanded he be allowed to remain an extra day so they could discuss business, and Lord Warwick agreed, though anyone could see he did not want to." He pursed his lips in evident anger. "I found the baron's request quite inconsiderate. The man's father was just murdered, after all!"

Vicky frowned. "I heard the marquess is a weak man, which is a shame, for he has a kind soul from what I have seen thus far."

"He does," James replied. "But I tell you, Kent certainly does not. As we fished, I tried to make inquiries, to gather any information that might prove useful. Sadly, I found nothing of importance save one thing."

"And what was that?"

"The acquisition and selling of land the baron mentioned? It includes this very estate. That was how the duke planned to fund his portion of the deal."

Vicky tapped her lips. "Lady Warwick said that the estate was to go to the duchess. Yet, that means that with the duke now dead — and with Lord Warwick's weak countenance…" She allowed her voice to trail off.

"Lord Gerard wishes to proceed with the purchase of Stanting Estate and leave the duchess without a home," James finished for her.

Chapter Eight

Of all the many questions left unanswered, certain ones rose above the rest in Vicky's mind, all pertaining to Mr. Richard Kent. He had lied to her about the time of his appointment, which he stated was after hers when in truth it had been scheduled an hour before. Which begged the question, why had he returned when he had?

Also, he had failed to mention his propensity to listen outside closed doors, a point that could save or drown him. What could he have hoped to learn by eavesdropping on Lord Gerard and the duchess when his meeting with the duke had already taken place? Unless he was already aware the two were having an affair and wished to use it as ammunition against His Grace.

At any rate, she would learn the truth once and for all.

"Do you know where I may find Mr. Kent?" she asked the butler.

"The last I saw of him was in the library, miss."

Vicky smiled. "Thank you."

Although her first inclination was to confront Mr. Kent outright, a new thought came to mind. The man had as much motive as anyone to murder the duke.

If he was indeed the culprit, perhaps he had gone to his room to hide the poison and then returned to see the results of his handiwork. That would explain his return to the study an hour past his appointed time when he could feign surprise at finding the duke dead.

What he had not expected was to find Vicky there, and therefore he concocted the story of having an appointment with the duke to explain his sudden appearance. The schedule had not been announced, after all.

Vicky gave a glance toward the library. There would be no better time for her to sneak upstairs to search the man's room than now. Therefore, she hurried up to the second floor, stopping and straining to hear any sounds coming from the hallway that housed the room assigned to Mr. Kent. Hearing none, she made her way down the hallway but stopped in front of the door leading to the duchess's rooms.

"Next month I will be one and twenty and a widow," the duchess said with a sigh. "Do you believe such a burden will age me?"

"Not at all, Your Grace," a female voice, perhaps that of a lady's maid, said. "You're much too beautiful to ever age."

"Tell me more about my beauty," the duchess said. Vicky could hear the smile she likely wore. "It will help ease my pain."

Shaking her head, Vicky tiptoed past the door and stopped before the door that led to Mr. Kent's room. How would she do this without being caught? She had never entered the bedroom of another with the sole purpose of prying. Would this now make her a criminal?

Taking a deep breath, she turned the handle and peeked inside.

The room was like her own, although where her walls were a light blue, these were beige. A large bed sat against one wall and a mirrored table sat against another. A large window allowed the rays of the sun to filter through the bubbled glass.

Taking one last glance to ascertain that no one was coming, Vicky slipped into the room. She hurried to the wardrobe but stopped to bite her lip. By searching his belongings, she was invading Mr. Kent's privacy. Yet, her reasoning trumped his rights, or so she justified. What she did was important work, and if the man had not lied, she would have had no reason to investigate him thus.

Feeling better, she pulled open the wardrobe. It was empty.

Drat!

She glanced around the room and her eyes fell on a bag that sat on a chair. Leave it to a man to leave his belongings packed! She rummaged through the bag but found no bottle of poison or anything indicating he committed murder.

What she did find was a letter. With a racing heart, she opened it and began to read. It was from the duke. The first paragraph contained an invitation much like hers to come to the estate this weekend. However, where hers had stopped there, this letter continued.

Although I have considered many ways I will pay my debt to you, I believe I have arrived at a satisfactory method to meet my obligation that I believe you will appreciate. A Miss Victoria Parker will be in attendance at the gathering, a woman of great beauty any gentleman would acknowledge upon seeing her. You will let me know if she suffices as payment...

Bile rose in Vicky's throat, but she had no time to consider what she had read, for Richard's voice rose from out in the corridor. She pushed the letter back into the bag and hurried over to the window. Climbing out was out of the question. If she were to fall, her chances of survival were slim. However, she could not be caught in Richard's room!

In a panic, she dropped to her stomach and slithered beneath the bed just as the door opened.

The door clicked shut, and Vicky prayed the man would retrieve whatever he came to collect and leave.

She glanced around her with wide eyes. *Please, let there be no spiders!* her harried brain screamed as it pictured a giant arachnid spinning a cocoon around her and holding her in place before sucking all the blood out of her. Few things frightened her, but spiders made up for every other fear she could have possessed. Fortunately, the underneath of the bed had been swept clean of any cobwebs.

Richard's feet appeared beside the bed and then the mattress sank. There was not much room beneath the bed, and she could feel the straw of the bottom mattress poke through her dress, making her back itch.

With just enough room to move her head to the side, she stared at the polished boots now spattered with bits of mud.

Had the duke planned on allowing this man to kidnap her? That was the only conceivable way she could be used to pay a gambling debt, for she would certainly not have agreed to any terms that would have her coupled with Richard Kent.

"If there were but a priest," Richard murmured, "I would stop myself from killing her. Yet, I have no choice. She must die."

Vicky held her breath. Was he speaking of the duchess? Or perhaps it was Lady Warwick. She strained to listen further.

Mr. Kent sighed. "I have no choice," he continued. "I must kill Miss Victoria Parker now."

Placing a hand over her mouth — not an easy task with her limited mobility — Vicky swallowed a scream.

The bed creaked, and the mattress rose once more before his shoes disappeared from sight. The door opened and closed and then there was silence.

She lay there for a moment in shock. Richard Kent wished to kill her? That meant she was on the right path to finding the murderer. And it had to be him.

She had to search out the constable as soon as possible, after informing James first, of course. If she did not do something soon, she would be as dead as the duke.

Sliding from beneath the bed, she stood and glanced down at her dress. The floor was not as clean as she first thought, and she batted at the fabric to rid herself of the dust that had gathered on her front.

When she turned to leave, her eyes went wide, and before she could scream, a hand clapped over her mouth.

"Hello, Victoria," Richard Kent said with a smile that did not reach his eyes. "What are you doing in my room?"

Vicky thought her heart would burst from her chest. This was it. She was going to die, and no one would find her body until Richard was long gone from the estate.

"Now, will you remain quiet when I remove my hand? If you scream, I may have to take drastic measures."

Given no choice, Vicky nodded. When he removed his hand, she took a step back. "It does not matter why I am here," she said, unsure from where this bout of courage came. "I heard your confession!"

Richard inched closer, grinning like the ghoul he was. "Did you?"

"Stay back or I shall scream!" Vicky took another step back, but the back of her legs bumped into the side of the bed, causing her to involuntarily sit upon it.

"Go ahead," Richard said, leering over her. "Everyone will come only to find you sitting upon my bed. Surely they will wonder what you are doing here." He offered a hand. "May I offer a bit of advice that may serve you well in the days ahead?"

Vicky managed to give a strained "yes". So, he did not plan to murder her immediately. At least she had time to stop him. If she was able.

"The next time you decide to hide beneath a bed, make certain your feet are not sticking out." He raised a single eyebrow. "I must admit that I was unsure who would do such a thing, but it did not take long to realize it was you."

"It could have been another woman," Vicky said with indignation. "How did you know it was me?"

"Two things led to my conclusion," Richard replied. "The first was the hint of blue on your dress. I admired it earlier this morning. The second was the lovely stockings on your ankle. They would leave any man breathless."

Richard offered his hand once more, and Vicky accepted it, although reluctantly. Then she gasped as he pulled her to her feet and promptly wrapped his arms around her waist.

He gazed down at her, a mischievous grin on his face. "I admit that the sight will fuel my dreams for years to come."

"Mr. Kent!" Vicky said in a harsh whisper as she yanked his arms from around her, "I have never been spoken to so crudely. Please remember you are supposed to be a gentleman."

Richard laughed. "It is because I am a gentleman that I ask you again, why are you in my room?"

Vicky's mind churned. "I-I was confused," she stammered. "I thought this was my room. By the time I realized it was not, I heard your voice and hid."

"Plausible," Richard said, "but unlikely." He began to unbutton his coat.

The room began to spin. Was the man a rogue? Of course he was. He had kissed her knuckles earlier and made a comment about her ankles!

"Mr. Kent, I may not be a lady of noble birth, but I am a woman with morals," she stated with as much outrage as she could muster. "If you believe I shall remain while you undress, you are sorely mistaken."

Richard laid his coat on the bed went to his bag. "Do not believe yourself so lucky," he said. "I can see the desire in your eyes, but I am not easily fooled by this innocent act you perform."

How dare he! "My innocence is no act," she said, her hands on her hips. "Now, if you do not mind – or even if you do – I will leave."

Glancing down, Richard pulled out the letter she had hastily returned to his bag. "This is not how I left it," he said as he allowed the parchment to fall to the floor. "I will ask you one more time, Victoria, and please do not lie. Why are you here?"

Seeing there was no way out except to speak the truth, Vicky heaved a frustrated sigh. "Oh, very well. I came to search your room for any indication as to why you lied about last night."

"I lied?" Richard asked with raised brows. "About what did I lie?"

"That you had an appointment with the duke just after mine," she replied. "I have come to learn that it was an hour earlier." She said the last with a firm nod. "I came across that letter in my search. I see that the duke expected to use me as some form of payment for his gambling debt to you. However, how the duke — or you for that matter — would believe I would give myself to you is simply absurd. You would have to kidnap me."

Her breath came in short gasps such was her anger. No man laid claim to her heart, and no one, even Richard or the duke, would speak on her behalf. The fact they believed they could only fueled her anger further.

"You?" Richard said, laughing. "Payment for a gambling debt? And you believe I would lower myself to kidnapping someone to get what I want?" He clutched his stomach as he tumbled to the bed in laughter. "Women are so vain! And you more so than most!" He sat up and wiped at his eyes. "I take it you did not read the entire letter."

"Well, no," she replied. "I did not have time."

He reached down to collect the parchment from where it had dropped. "Allow me to read it to you," he said. "'Although I have considered many ways I will pay my debt to you, I believe I have arrived at a satisfactory method to meet my obligation that I believe you will appreciate. A Miss Victoria Parker will be in attendance at the gathering, a woman of great beauty any gentleman would acknowledge upon seeing her. You will let me know if she suffices as payment.'" He paused and looked up at her. "I assume that was where you stopped reading."

She nodded but could not speak.

He chuckled and continued on. "'I believe that once an introduction is made, the two of you will find one another's company satisfactory. You must understand that her father was a man I greatly respected, and therefore, I also respect her. I ask that you remain a gentleman in her presence and that you not make me regret my decision to introduce the two of you.'" Richard refolded the letter and set it aside. "I must say that the man was right. You are a woman of great beauty. However, I may be many things, but a kidnapper is not one of them, I assure you."

"But the night of the duke's murder," Vicky said, "you said he owed you a debt and that now he was dead, he would be unable to pay it."

"Indeed," Richard replied. "And I have no reason to think otherwise, for how do you get money from a dead man? Now that he is not here to make the necessary introductions, I have vowed to learn who killed him. You see, I am not the cad you believe me to be. I would prefer a proper introduction. You, on the other hand, seem to have no need for such formalities. And as for my appointment?" He pulled a scrap of parchment from the inside pocket of his coat and handed it to her. "You will see there that he asked me to return in order to meet you."

Five past midnight, had been scrawled on the paper.

Vicky was speechless. It appeared she had made a mistake in her judgment of this man. He was much more gallant than she had first believed. Yet, with his reputation, how else was she supposed to think of him?

What bothered her most was that she had trusted the duke, believed him to see her as more than a female assistant in her father's office. That, too, had been a mistake. He was no different from any other man who saw women as nothing more than a slab of meat to be traded as currency.

"You overheard Lord Gerard and the duchess speaking in the library," she said, moving the conversation to a more comfortable topic. "What did you hear?"

Richard frowned. "How did you know about that?"

"Lady Warwick mentioned it. Did you not see her?"

"I saw someone in the shadows, but the person fled before I could identify who it was. But in regard to me eavesdropping, I admit that I was."

"And what did you hear?" she asked again.

"They were discussing the business deal that the duke mentioned at dinner," Richard replied. "The duchess assured Lord Gerard that she would see it happen. I believe she sealed it with a kiss."

"How would you know that?"

He laughed. "I do know the sound of a kiss, Victoria."

Feeling her face heat, Vicky attempted to bring the conversation around once more. "But that makes no sense. If the deal were to go through, she would have no home to inherit. How else would she afford to invest?"

"True," Richard replied, "But I suspect there is more here than meets the eye. The duchess has a way of swaying Lord Warwick. Perhaps she plans to get him to find other funds for the investment. Then she would not be forced to sell the estate."

"But why is this venture so important to her?"

Richard smiled. "Because she plans to marry the baron."

Vicky gasped. "Are you certain?"

"Quite certain," he replied. "I have long suspected they were having an affair, and last night confirmed it. Her plan is genius yet simple. Allow me to explain."

"There is no need," Vicky said. "For you are correct; it is simple." She ignored his frown. "By having the duke killed, the duchess will retain the estate. The baron then convinces Lord Warwick to follow through with the deal his father wished to vacate, which in turn adds more funds to the baron's coffers. When he marries the duchess, both of their wealth increases." She gathered her skirts and turned toward the door. "I must speak to Lord Gerard and the duchess," she said. "Thank you for verifying what I already knew. It only strengthens my case."

As she went to open the door, however, Richard placed his hand on it. "I now trust you," he said. "Do you trust me?"

"I believe you spoke the truth about what happened last night and why, yes," she replied. "However, that does not mean I trust you in other areas."

He snorted and moved away from the door, allowing her to open it.

She peeked in both directions and, seeing no one, walked into the corridor.

"Victoria," Richard whispered. She turned a glare on him. "Perhaps when this is all over, you will allow me to call on you."

"That would be nice," she replied in her most docile tone. When his smile widened, she added, "Unfortunately, I am quite busy. For the next fifty years." With that, she walked away, pleased that his smug grin had been wiped from his face.

James approached, and she smiled at him. She had so much to tell him! He came to a sudden stop, glared at her, and then turned on his heel and hurried away.

She frowned. What was wrong with him?

It was not until he was out of sight that it occurred to her what he must have been thinking. He had just seen her leave Richard's room and sneak down the hallway as if she had done something terribly wrong. And the very thought of what he suspected broke her heart.

Chapter Nine

Vicky caught a glimpse of James entering the library as she reached the bottom of the stairs. Worry guided her steps as she thought about what the man must think of her. And who could blame him? She had been caught coming out of a man's room, which was appalling in itself. It was not just any man, however. It was Richard Kent, known swindler and wooer of women if rumor was to be believed. And Vicky believed those rumors wholeheartedly.

At the now-closed door, Vicky drew in a calming breath. She would explain the reason why she had gone to Richard's room, that she had been forced to hide, and that nothing was amiss. All she had to do then was pray James believed her.

Yet, as she reached for the handle, she paused. What if James told her he wanted nothing more to do with her? The mere thought of her friend not being near filled her with a sense of dread and sorrow, and if anyone were to ask her, she would not have been able to explain why.

This was silly! She sounded like a love-sick girl! Surely her misgivings stemmed from the fact they had become close friends since the passing of her father, for it had been James who had been at her side, supporting her at every turn. His friendship was what she had come to cherish and not some form of romantic attachment.

With renewed purpose, she turned the handle and entered the library. James stood before one of the many bookshelves that filled the room, all of which reached from floor to a ceiling so high, one needed a ladder to reach the uppermost shelves. There were so many books in the room, Vicky wondered how the poor maids kept up the dusting of them. Or rather that was what she would have wondered if she had not been so focused on James.

She eased the door closed and went to stand beside her friend, who stared at a book open in his hands.

"I must speak to you concerning what you saw," she whispered. After learning about Richard and Lady Warwick's eavesdropping, she could not take any chances someone might overhear. "The reason I went there was—"

"There is no need to explain," James said. "I am merely your assistant and therefore you have no reason to explain anything to me." He returned the book to its place without looking at her.

"That may well be true on the surface," she said, hurrying over to him, "but your opinion of me means a great deal. I am not what you believe me to be."

James turned toward her, his eyes searching hers. "Who do I believe you to be?" he asked.

Vicky glanced down as shame washed over her. "A spinster caught in a man's room. There are words for women like that."

"And you believe after all these years I would think of you in that way?" he asked in a soft tone.

His question caught her off-guard, and for a moment she could say nothing in response as he returned to his perusal of the books.

Vicky placed a hand on his arm. "You are right. I know you think better of me than that. Regardless, I would like to explain what you saw."

James closed the book with a sigh. "Why? To clear your name?"

She nodded. "Yes, of course."

"Vicky, there is nothing to explain to me. Not now, not ever."

"Then why are you acting as if you are upset with me?" she asked.

"The look you gave me in the hallway was one of disgust. If you do not wish to tell me for fear I will dismiss you, you are quite mistaken. I value your opinion." Her face heated. "Even if I may not like what I hear."

"It is not that."

"Then please, tell me what it is."

He turned toward her. "When I saw you leave his room, for a moment I was angry. Not with you but myself."

"Yourself?" she asked, taken aback.

James shoved the book into its place on the shelf as if it had wronged him in some way. "This is a mistake. Let us discuss something else."

He went to move past her, but Vicky grabbed his arm. "Do not leave me like this. Tell me what upset you so I can repair whatever has broken."

His sad expression confused her further. "When I saw you leaving his room, I admit I was hurt. The idea of you being with a man, even if it is to talk with him, bothers me, for I am well aware the day will come when you find someone who makes you happy. And although it will bring you the joy you deserve, it will hurt me."

Vicky stood in shock. How could she not have recognized how James felt toward her? She had never thought of him in an intimate way…

No, that was untrue. There had been fleeting moments when his smile warmed her heart, or his laughter made her giddy. But that was not love. She had no doubt James would treat her with the respect he had always shown if they were to pursue another avenue together, but she had dared to take that path once in her life. That had led to disaster, and the thought of enduring such anguish again made her push any and all feelings of admiration she might feel for any man into the recesses of her mind.

"I appreciate very much what you have said," she said, choosing her words carefully. "And as my friend—"

"And your friend I will always be," he said over her words. "There is nothing more to discuss. Now, tell me what you learned from Kent."

There was no sense arguing with him when he became this stubborn, so Vicky decided it would be best if they continued later with this topic.

She explained the conversation she and Richard had shared. When she was done, her heart hurt upon seeing a remnant of sadness in James's eyes.

"I will attempt to speak to Lord Warwick later," he said and then paused. "Perhaps I can seek him out now."

"Before you go, I believe it is important—"

The door opened and a maid entered the room, bobbing a quick curtsy. "Beggin' your pardon, sir, miss, but the constable's askin' for your attendance."

"Thank you," Vicky replied. With a glance at James, she walked out into the corridor and was surprised to find Lady Warwick waiting.

"I see you have been summoned, as well."

"Indeed," Vicky replied. She could not help but wonder how long the marchioness had been standing outside the door. Had the woman listened at the keyhole as she had the previous night? If so, what had she overheard?

Vicky had no time to wonder further, for by the time they arrived at their destination, the remaining guests, as well as their hostess, were already seated. Lord Warwick directed them to the couch where Richard sat, and Vicky made certain James sat between them.

Constable Cogwell stood before the fireplace, his hands clasped behind his back, and once James sat, he began.

"Now that we are all here, I would like to share what I have learned thus far. It appears His Grace kept a large staff within and without the confines of the house, which gives a great number of people who had access to him."

Richard chuckled and Lord Gerard gave such a loud yawn, Vicky feared it would shatter the windows.

The constable either did not hear or chose to ignore them. "I have spoken to everyone who works outside the great house — the stable hands, groomsmen, gardeners, and such — and after a brief nap, I will begin my inquiries with those who are employed within."

As the man droned, Vicky's mind began to wander. She glanced at James. If any man was worthy of love, it was he. He possessed a kind heart and his actions were gentlemanly despite his lack of title or station. He also had a handsomeness about him.

Would pursuing any sort of romantic relationship with a man she deemed a good friend be worth the chance of being hurt again? Not likely. Plus, their friendship would be left in tatters. No, as enticing as it seemed, she could not risk it, for she would end up hurting him as she had once been hurt.

"Cogwell," Lord Gerard said, standing. Vicky had not even noticed when the constable had ceased his lecture. "There is none here who would doubt your sincerity in regard to this inquest. However, I fear we shall starve before you complete it." He turned to the marquess. "George, do you not believe it would be best if we ate now so the constable may continue with whatever it is he must do?"

Vicky stared at the baron. Did he just address the new duke by his Christian name? Were they that close and Vicky had not realized? She glanced around at the other attendees. They, too, were gaping at him. All except Lord Warwick.

"You are right," Lord Warwick replied. "Food and rest are the order of the day, for the loss of my father in such a horrible manner has been troubling for us all. Thank you, my friend."

Lady Warwick, whose eyes were nearly popping out of her head, said, "My husband, do not apologize. You will soon be the duke."

"He will only have that position because my husband is dead!" the duchess said as she placed the back of her hand to her forehead. "My heart is breaking all over again because of you, Lavinia!"

Lord Gerard hurried to her side and took hold of her hand. "This lady needs fresh air. I will escort Her Grace at once. George, please open the door for her."

Vicky watched in astonishment as the soon-to-be duke leaped from his chair and practically ran to do the baron's bidding like an obedient servant. Lady Warwick also jumped from her seat, scolding her husband as she followed him out of the room.

One by one, the remaining guests made their way to the dining room. Vicky followed James, who had yet to look her way, nor did he offer her his arm.

Waiting at the door was Lady Warwick, and as Vicky moved to walk past her, the marchioness caught her by the arm and led her aside. "May I request a favor?"

"Of course," Vicky replied. "Whatever you need."

"I fear Charlotte should not be alone with Lord Gerard. Go and find her for me, will you, please?"

Of the many things Vicky wished to do at this very moment, searching out the duchess was very far down on the list. "I will do so now," Vicky found herself saying with great reluctance. While one did not simply go in search of a duchess who wished to not be disturbed, one also did not deny a soon-to-be duchess any request, either.

***

A sweeping glance of the gardens showed no one, which left the couple likely behind any one of the many rows of hedges. Resigning herself to searching them out lest she came under the scorn of Lady Warwick, Vicky made her way down the cobblestone path.

Glancing to her right, she caught sight of the baron and the duchess as they made a left down a far path that led away from the house. Vicky hurried after them, tall carefully trimmed hedges on either side of her, and paused at the end of the path to listen. Unfortunately, their voices were nothing more than hushed whispers, and she could not discern any of their words.

Vicky made her way to the edge of the closest bush and dared to peek around the corner, and what she saw made her pull back. The duchess was in Lord Gerard's embrace! Taking several deep breaths to slow her racing heart, she glanced around the corner again.

"Do not worry," the baron said. "All will be well soon enough."

To Vicky's horror, Lord Gerard looked her way, and she took a quick step back. Her foot caught on a protruding root, which promptly sent her toppling to the ground, leaving her bottom smarting. A moment later, the baron came around the corner, his face crinkled in anger.

"What are you doing here?" he demanded. "Were you spying on me?"

"Spying?" Vicky squeaked. "No, of course not, my lord." She took the hand he offered her and stood. "Lady Warwick requested I go in search of Her Grace," Vicky continued as she brushed at her skirts. "Then I spotted the most ghastly of creatures scurrying across the path. It gave me such a fright, I lost my footing in my attempt to escape and that was how I ended up on the ground."

The baron narrowed his eyes at her as if doubting her words. "Charlotte has already returned to the house," he said. "I suggest you do the same."

Vicky glanced past him. Indeed, the duchess was gone. She had not even seen the woman leave, her embarrassment had been so great.

As Lord Gerard went to move past her, Vicky said, "You love her, do you not?" Bluntness was not the best way to garner information, but this might be the only chance she had to speak to the baron alone.

"Do you speak of Charlotte?" the baron asked, his back to her.

"Indeed," Vicky replied. "I realize it is none of my business—"

"And yet you choose to interfere anyway." He turned to face her, his features dark with anger. "Tell me, Miss Parker, what is it you wish to learn by asking me such a question?"

With no other alternative than to speak the truth, Vicky replied, "I learned you were in the library with Her Grace then night the duke was murdered."

"I was," he replied. "I will not deny that such a meeting took place. If my memory serves correctly, it was around eleven. I had already met with the duke, and Her Grace was awaiting her appointment."

"May I ask the topic of your discussion?" Vicky asked. She doubted he would respond, but it was her hope he would feel the need to clear the air.

Lord Gerard barked a laugh that made Vicky feel as if she was a tiny as the creatures that scurried beneath the rocks. "You are the daughter of an accountant – and a spinster to boot – and you dare believe it wise to question a baron?"

Vicky was uncertain whether the sudden sense of frustration that came over her stemmed from the lies she had heard throughout the day or if it was due to the arrogance of the man who stood before her. Regardless, she snapped an answer that came directly from her heart.

"I ask because a great man died while you were alone with his wife in the library. That alone gives me a reason to inquire."

She steeled herself for his rebuttal but was surprised when he simply smiled and replied, "Very well, Miss Parker. Come. Walk with me and I will tell you what you wish to know." He turned and walked further down the path, and Vicky had to hasten her steps to catch up to him. "For many years, Warwick — the father, mind you — and I have engaged in matters of business. The latest venture required more than six months of hard work on my part just to set it in place. You see, my time is precious to me, equally as precious as the money I have spent drawing up this deal."

"Yet you became angry with the duke," Vicky said. "At dinner last evening, you did nothing to hide your disappointment."

"And because I am disappointed you believe I would kill a friend?" he asked with a laugh. "I suppose that would make for some wonderful gossip amongst the *ton*. I already fear what the servants must be saying. But I assure you, that is not true. The truth is that the duchess and I were speaking of business before I escorted her to her rooms, where I left her at the door. Now you have the exciting gossip you need."

Vicky came to a stop. "My lord, I heard the duchess did not wish to go to India, nor did she wish to see this estate sold in order to fund her husband's venture."

"Of course she did not wish to see her home sold," Lord Gerard replied. "She has come to love this place, and as the mistress of the house, she has every right to be upset about it. Most women would be if they were in her position."

"That is true," Vicky conceded. "Is that why you have asked Lord Warwick to use his funds to back your venture? So the duchess would retain Stanting Estate?"

"It is."

Vicky waited for him to elaborate, but he only stared down at her. It was the next question that had her stomach in knots. However, after what she had witnessed between the baron and the duchess while they were alone together, she had to inquire. "I also heard that the two of you have developed a relationship with one another, one that goes beyond simple friendship."

Rather than anger, Vicky was met with amusement. "Charlotte and I?" he asked. "That simply is untrue. We are friends and nothing more, I assure you."

Vicky was uncertain if she believed him, but what had she expected? A baron had no reason to reveal the truth to the likes of an accountant's daughter.

"The man who arrived with you," the baron said. "Kensington, is that correct?"

"It is," Vicky replied, wondering what this had to do with the answers she sought. "James Kensington."

"And he controls your father's business?"

Vicky nodded.

"I imagine that the two of you spend a great deal of time alone together during the course of your work, do you not?"

"Well, yes, of course, but—"

Lord Gerard raised a hand to forestall her. "Allow me to finish, Miss Parker. It is rude to interrupt. Now, where was I? Oh, yes. The two of you alone. And the journey here? You traveled together, am I correct in saying so?"

Vicky nodded again.

"One may deduce that the two of you are lovers. Or are you merely friends working toward a common goal? Which should I believe?"

"That we are only friends, my lord," Vicky replied.

"Then I would request the same consideration be given to Charlotte and me. Once this deal with George is completed, I will take over whatever allowance Her Grace receives and manage it for her. As one with intimate knowledge of business dealings would do for a friend who lacks the education on how to best use the funds left to her."

Vicky could only stand in silence. Besides the rumors she had heard, and the conclusions she had made, there was no proof the two were romantically involved. Granted, she had seen them embracing, but the duchess had been quite upset when she left. Perhaps he was consoling her and nothing more.

"Now, if you are done with your inquest," the baron snapped, "we should join the others."

"One more question, if I may." Vicky ignored Lord Gerard's frown. "Did the duchess encourage you to present the duke with a bottle of brandy in order to gain his approval?"

The baron blanched. "Are you insinuating that it was I – or God forbid, the duchess – who poisoned His Grace?"

"Miss Parker?" a voice called out before Vicky could respond. She turned to see Lady Warwick come around the corner.

"There you are," the marchioness said. "I thought you had disappeared. What are you doing here?"

"I was speaking with—" She glanced down the now-empty path. The baron was gone.

"I appreciate you looking after Charlotte," Lady Warwick said. "She returned to the house safely. Now, come. We have a delicious luncheon prepared for us." She slipped her arm through Vicky's and gave a cheerful smile. "I am sure you will enjoy it as much as I."

Chapter Ten

"Ah, Miss Parker," Richard Kent said when Vicky and Lady Warwick entered the dining room. "I have reserved a seat beside me for you."

Vicky considered whether it would be prudent to fall over and feign death rather than join the man. Tempting fate, she took the seat he offered.

"And that is why tonight I have arranged to have a string quartet play for us in the ballroom," Lord Warwick was saying to the others. His face dropped. "It was meant to celebrate Father's journey to India, but now perhaps we can use it to signal a new era without him. We shall have an evening of indulgence, mark my words."

Vicky shivered at the sudden chill that filled the room as a footman placed a plate filled with smoked salmon, three types of cheeses, and blanched carrots before her.

"If you had not always encouraged the duke to drink," the duchess said, pouting, "he would still be alive. Perhaps it was not poison but rather his love of the drink itself that caused his untimely death."

Lady Warwick's utensils clicked as she slammed them against her plate. "Must you blame everything on George? It never ceases to amaze me…"

Richard leaned in close and whispered, "We must speak alone soon. It is important and I fear it cannot wait much longer."

"Oh?" Vicky asked, doing her best to appear uninterested in what he had to say. There was no need to draw everyone's eyes away from the argument between the duchess and the marchioness. "Have you learned something new?"

"I cannot tell you here. Make an excuse to leave the table and I will follow."

Vicky nodded.

Lord Warwick rose from his seat and the room fell instantly quiet. "We must have faith the constable will learn who murdered my father. Arguing with one another will not help matters in the slightest. Please, keep a civil tongue, both of you."

The duchess sighed. "You are right, George," she replied. "I will ignore those who seek to disrupt our meal." She gave the marchioness a smug smile.

Lady Warwick sniffed. "My husband is wise, as he always is. Let us ignore those who seek to place their guilt upon others."

Seeing no better time to sneak away, Vicky excused herself and hurried from the room. No one seemed to notice. She made her way down the long corridor to the library. Not two minutes later, Richard entered the room.

"So," she said, hurrying over to him, "what have you learned?"

Richard drew in a deep breath. "My mind has been consumed with a fact that has bothered me greatly."

Vicky nodded, urging the man to continue.

"When George becomes the duke, he will be well-respected by many."

"Of course he will," Vicky replied and then paused. "Do you believe he murdered his father for that very motive?"

"I am unsure," Richard said. "But do you not see? I can have the new duke introduce us formally. Surely such an invitation from a man of his position will give you a reason to agree to allow me to call on you."

Vicky gritted her teeth. "You took me away from a lovely meal in hopes that I will give you permission to call on me?"

"I did."

"Mr. Kent, I have never seen such foolishness in my life. A man was murdered, and your mind is on how to use it to your advantage?"

"Is it not wonderful?" he asked with a grin. "I could not have planned it better myself! Even in the midst of a murder, I think only of you!"

There was no time to stand here listening to such twaddle. "I am going to return to the dining room, for the company there is far more desirable than you could ever be!" She turned on her heel and walked toward the door.

"I did hear something that may interest you."

Vicky stopped and closed her eyes. "If this is about—"

"You?" he asked. "Please, do not be so vain."

Vicky turned and narrowed her eyes, willing the bookshelf beside him to topple over and burying him alive. It would be a fitting end!

"But before I tell you," Richard said, "what did you learn about the baron? I assume you spoke to him."

"He admitted to being with the duchess that night, but he says they are nothing more than friends. In fact—"

"Friends?" Richard asked with a laugh. "Gerard has no friends, only those he uses to get what he wants. But please, go on."

"If you would stop interrupting me, I would be grateful," Vicky said. Richard pretended to button his lip, and she continued. "Thank you. That is all I know. Now, what have you learned."

His smile grew mischievous. "You know more than you are letting on," he said. "And although I should keep what I heard to myself, I will tell you." He glanced at the lounge. "Would you care to sit?"

"What did you hear?" Vicky demanded. She was not here to be wooed by a scoundrel!

Richard shrugged. "When Lady Warwick sent you away, she spoke with her husband alone. I just happened to overhear her warning him."

"Warning him? About what?"

"That he was not to reveal to anyone that he had given his father the brandy," Richard replied, a triumphant grin on his face. "And, if need be, they would blame it on the butler."

Vicky could not help but gape. "So, it appears Lord Warwick may have taken advantage of that motive after all. Yet, there is one problem with your theory. The duke met with his son an hour before we found him dead, and Lady Warwick stated he was asleep well before midnight." Vicky sighed in frustration. The timelines of everyone's whereabouts collided with one another.

"That may be," Richard replied, "but that is unimportant at the moment. What is important is the fact that Lady Warwick does not want her husband to admit the brandy was a gift from him. I think that makes it perfectly clear who the murderer is. Now we only need to prove it."

Although Richard was correct, proving it would be difficult. In fact, it would be nearly impossible to get the man to confess. One thing was certain, Vicky would have to tread carefully so as not bring suspicion down around her ears.

***

Vicky returned to the dining room, hoping her absence had gone unnoticed. Unfortunately, as soon as she entered the room, she stopped. Everyone was gone, the table had been cleared, and the butler sat polishing the silver.

When he saw her, he stood. "May I help you, Miss Parker?"

Pulling out the chair opposite the butler, she waved him back to his seat. "There is no need to stand on my account," she said. "And where has everyone gone?"

"They have retired to their rooms to rest," the butler replied. "Is there anything I can get for you? Tea perhaps?"

"No, thank you…I am sorry, but what is your name?"

"Sheplin, miss."

"Have you been employed here long, Sheplin?"

"Quite a time, miss, yes. For forty years I have been in the service of His Grace, and now it is my hope I can continue with the son. The Sheplin family has served the Warwicks for over a hundred years, though I am afraid that once I am gone, there will be no others after me."

"Oh, I see," Vicky said. "You have no children, then?"

The butler snorted. "I have two sons, miss, but both are feeble-minded and would ruin a hundred years of good standing in one afternoon."

Vicky was uncertain how to respond to such a comment, so she merely smiled. Then it occurred to her that a family's butler could be a great source of information. "Sheplin, may I ask you something?"

"Of course, miss."

"The duchess mentioned that the duke and Lord Warwick often drank together. Is this true?"

"His Grace did enjoy a good brandy in the late evening, and oftentimes with a favored guest. However, Lord Warwick does not partake in any alcohol, which was a disappointment to His Grace." He leaned forward and lowered his voice. "I would say that Lord Warwick has disappointed his father in many ways."

"Oh?" Vicky asked with an air of conspiratorial interest. "I had no idea!"

"And you wouldn't, miss," Sheplin replied. "Unless you were a part of the family, which you are not. You see, Lord Warwick has spent most of his life living very differently from his peers. He prefers to concentrate on charity rather than business. As his peers hunted foxes, Lord Warwick attended the theater. Three years ago, he wished to audition for a role in one of the plays, if you can believe it! Can you imagine the shame the duke would have endured? His own flesh and blood performing on a stage?"

In Vicky's opinion there were worse ways a son could embarrass his father, including murder, yet she nodded agreement, nonetheless. "I heard His Grace died from poisoning," she whispered as she glanced toward the doorway. "I wish I knew who would do such a terrible thing."

"Miss Parker, every guest here had something to gain from the duke's death. To speculate who gains the most is futile, for it is only a matter of perspective. One person's gain does not carry equal weight to the next."

"I must admit that I have been making inquiries into the death of the duke," Vicky said. "I fear the constable lacks a certain...capacity, let us say, in drawing conclusions."

The butler snorted. "I would not think that is the reason for his inability to solve this crime, miss."

"Why is that?"

"Because the duchess has already paid him off."

Vicky leaned back in her chair and gaped.

"Do not act so surprised, Miss Parker. Such actions are commonplace among the nobility."

"Then you believe the duchess—"

"I believe only what I know and see," Sheplin said. "And I watched her with my own eyes pay the man to look elsewhere. Now, if you have nothing more to ask me, I have work to do."

"One last thing," Vicky said. "Last evening, everyone claims they were asleep when the duke was murdered. Did you see anything out of the ordinary?"

The butler let out a long sigh and placed the fork and polishing rag on the table. "You do realize that a murderer is among us, do you not?" he asked, clasping his gloved hands in front of him. "And there is no reason he — or she — may not strike again."

Vicky's heart pounded. "Are you threatening me?"

"Why would I—? Ah, I see. I am not the murderer, Miss Parker. That position belongs to another. What I mean to say is that you should be careful making inquiries, for if you get too close, someone may wish to remove you, too."

"I do understand that," Vicky replied. "However, the duke was always kind to my father and me, and I cannot allow the murderer to go free."

"Then allow me to tell you this," the butler said. "As the guests waited for their appointment, some met in the sitting room while others went off alone. No one was asleep at midnight when the alarm was raised, contrary to what they may tell you. I saw them all with my own eyes, even those who were together."

"You must be speaking about the duchess and Lord Gerard."

"Not at all," Sheplin replied. "I speak of Mr. Kent and Lady Warwick."

Vicky felt as if the air had been removed from her lungs. Richard and the marchioness? Could it be the two conspired together? Were they having an affair and planned the murder for some nefarious gain? It would not have surprised her in the least, not when it concerned Richard Kent.

"Do not look so astounded, Miss Parker," the butler said. "Although he would never have admitted it, I fear the duke had his suspicions."

"If that is true, then Mr. Kent could have poisoned the duke."

Sheplin chuckled as he gathered his cleaning materials and placed them on a tray. "Miss Parker, do you not see? The poison was meant to kill two, but it only killed one."

And with that, the butler left the room, leaving Vicky to decipher his riddle. It was not long before everything fell into place. She just had one more question to ask Lord Warwick to confirm her suspicions.

Chapter Eleven

The house was eerily quiet, and although she was a guest, Vicky could not help but feel as if she were more an intruder. Perhaps it was silly to believe such things, but as she walked toward the study, the sensation was unshakable.

Before she reached the room, the door opened and James exited, followed by Lord Gerard and Lord Warwick. The men spoke for a brief moment in hushed tones, and then James and the baron left, leaving the marquess behind.

That man caught sight of Vicky and said, "Ah, Miss Parker. Please, join me. There are matters I wish to discuss with you."

Vicky swallowed hard. Did he suspect she knew more than she should? Was the invitation to join him a way to get her alone to warn her about the power he held and the torment he could rain down on her for interfering with his well-placed plans?

"Miss Parker?"

"My apologies, my lord," Vicky said, shaking the thoughts from her head before curtsying. "My mind was elsewhere, a horrible habit that I have been meaning to correct." She gave him her best smile to further placate him. If he was the murderer, it was best if she stayed in his good graces or she could very well become his next victim.

Rather than showing anger, Lord Warwick returned her smile. "There is no need for apologies. With all that has transpired, none of us can think properly." He extended his arm to allow her to enter before him. The sound of the door closing did nothing to placate her fears. "Please, sit."

Vicky went to a large chair that faced the desk as Lord Warwick walked around and sat on the other side.

"You seem nervous," he said. "And I know why."

"You do?" Vicky croaked through a tight throat. Her worst fears had been realized. She had prodded the proverbial beehive and now the bees were going to attack.

"Indeed," Lord Warwick replied. "You believe you must be on guard while in my presence, especially now that I will take over my father's title. However, I assure you that I may be a Warwick, but I am not one to hold myself above others. We should treat one another as friends, for that is what we are, are we not?"

"Are we, my lord?" Vicky asked, dubious. She did not believe them to be enemies, but friends? That was taking things a bit further than someone of her station would expect.

"Why, yes, of course," Lord Warwick insisted. "And because I see us as friends, I think it was about time you addressed me as George. In private of course, and only if you feel comfortable doing so."

The confusion and uneasiness Vicky had been feeling only intensified as she nodded. "I suppose I can do that...George." The name stuck to her tongue, but she managed to get it out. Somehow.

"And I will address you as Victoria," he said with a smile. "James will be able to fill you in on the details later, but I have retained the services of your office for my accounting needs."

This surprised Vicky. "Thank you. That is very kind of you."

George leaned back into his seat. "I met your father once when I was but a boy. My father and I visited his office, and I could tell instantly that he was a very good man."

"He was, indeed," Vicky replied, a sentimental tug at her heart catching her breath. "There were none he did not consider a friend, and the word 'stranger' did not exist in his vocabulary."

"Such men are who I strive to be." George sighed. "Lavinia believes people mock me as weak, and in truth many do, but I believe a duke should do more than simply host parties or purchase fine horseflesh. He should look after those in his care, regardless of their station."

Vicky was uncertain in which direction the conversation was heading, but she knew where it needed to go. "My condolences for the loss of your father. Were you able to speak to him before he died?"

"I met with him at eleven," George said. Then he shook his head. "He scheduled an appointment with me just as he had every evening after dinner. You see, since I was a child, Father would bring me into his study and explain how I had failed him that day." A flicker of pain crossed his eyes. "Last night was no different. Of course, he let me know that others would be entrusted with the estate, but his wishes will no longer be fulfilled. I will prove to everyone that I am much more capable than he, or anyone else, believes by building upon his legacy how I see fit."

Vicky smiled. "He would be proud of your strength and forethought."

To this, George guffawed. "My father had no trust in me when it came to business. Or anything else for that matter. However, I have agreed to the deal that Father refused with Gerard, so now I will prove that I am a duke who is greater than my father. All my friends will see it, my family, even my wife will realize I am not the fool they believe me to be." His voice grew more feverish with each word, and by the time he finished, he was breathing heavily as if he had run a race.

"Well, I can assure you," Vicky said, "I do not think you a fool. In fact, I believe you will do well and prove your doubters wrong." She thought about what Sheplin had revealed to her. "I would be honored if you allow me to send you a bottle of brandy to celebrate your new business venture."

"That is a kind gesture, but I am afraid I must refuse. I do not partake in any form of spirits, though Father tried many times to convince me that no gentleman refused even the occasional drink. Every evening, during his moments of berating, he insisted I drink with him. Even last night, he made every attempt to share his brandy with me. Our meeting was not much different from any we had before, yet he was under the assumption I had changed my mind about sharing the brandy." He shook his head. "You would think a man would know his own son, but not him. I do not drink. Ever. It is as Sedgwick Fleming says, 'The drink that passes the lips soothes the tongue but troubles the soul'."

Vicky had no idea who Sedgwick Fleming was, nor did she care. She imagined George in this very room the previous night, the duke pleading with his son to drink. When the man gave up and took a drink for himself, did George watch as his father died before his very eyes?

"What did His Grace say last night when you refused him?" she asked.

"He threw me out if you can believe it," the marquess replied. "Told me I was unworthy of the dukedom, but then he always said that. No, I will go above and beyond what my father expected and show the world I am a greater duke than any of my predecessors."

"Then I can only offer you my congratulations and goodwill," she said. "Perhaps Lady Warwick would like a bottle of wine for herself?"

George snorted. "Lavinia drinks enough as it is," he said. "But you may send it all the same, for I will not refuse your goodwill twice." He turned to the window behind him. "She is outside now flaunting the gardens. She designed them, you know?"

"Oh?" Vicky said. "I did not know. Who is she with?"

"Kent," George replied. "Apparently, he is looking for inspiration for his own garden, which, between you and me, I find unbelievable."

Vicky inched closer in her chair. "Do you? Why so?"

A sly grin crossed his lips. "As I explained before, I am not the fool many believe me to be. It does not take much thought to know what they are likely doing at this very moment. I know they met last night in secret. Alone. And do you know why?"

Vicky grasped the arms of her chair, wanting to pull out her hair. Why must she be put in such a delicate situation? Whyever would this man wish Vicky to reveal the possibility of a romance budding between his wife and another man?

"It is all right, Vicky. You can tell me."

"I…that is…they are…" The words, although forming in her mind, refused to leave her lips. "You see, they are…"

George laughed so hard, Vicky jumped. "Planning a surprise for my birthday next month, are they not? Yes, I am well aware of their secret, for when I confronted Kent last evening as to why he was alone with my wife, he could do nothing but confess the truth to me." His grin was so wide, it nearly cut his face in two.

Vicky forced a smile. Was this clearly-oblivious man capable of planning the murder of anyone, let alone his own father? "Indeed, I heard much the same," she lied. "A celebration." Then a new question came to mind. Would the marquess admit that he gifted the duke the poisoned bottle? "The brandy your father drank last night? Do you know where he purchased it?"

His smile dropped and he hung his head. "It was a gift from me," he whispered. "I learned two months ago of his upcoming journey to India when I overheard him discussing it with a friend." A shiver ran down Vicky's spine as George's face reddened. "But I beg of you, do not let anyone know that I revealed that to you. Lavinia would be angry with me, and I have no desire to face her wrath."

"George," Vicky asked carefully, "did you wish your father—"

"I have some business I must attend to," he said with a smile that was forced, his chair scraping as he pushed it back. "Perhaps we can speak later."

Vicky rose and made her way to the door. Pausing, she glanced over to see the marquess sitting in his chair, which was turned toward the window behind him. He was nothing more than a boy, chastised by his father and all those around him. But even boys can cause mischief.

It was with this thought, Vicky set out in search of the constable. It was time she told him what she had learned. The thought saddened her, for George was an amiable man she did not wish to see hanged.

***

Having searched most of the common rooms and not encountering the constable, Vicky went to the kitchens to ask after him there. Upon entering the room, a heavyset woman with round cheeks and hands covered in flour looked Vicky up and down.

"Miss?" the woman asked.

"My apologies for disturbing you, but I am looking for Constable Cogwell. Have you seen him by chance?"

The woman snorted. "You mean the man who eats every hour on the hour?" she asked, pounding a fist into a ball of dough. "Just follow the food crumbs he leaves in his wake."

The door swung open and another woman entered the room. "Mrs. Prowler, I put in that order you asked."

The heavyset cook turned her head as she continued to knead the dough. "And was it right?" she demanded. "If Lady Warwick finds any mistakes with her order, we're all done for. And I got too much living left to do to be done for. You get me, girl?"

"I tell you, it was right," the younger woman insisted. "And I need my position just as much as you need yours." She turned on her heel and left the room in a huff.

Mrs. Prowler snorted a laugh. "Come work for the duke, they said. Good wages and fine food to enjoy, they said. Well, the wages are good enough, but the abuse I'm forced to endure to earn them isn't worth it."

Taken aback by the forwardness of the cook, Vicky said, "Is that so? Surely with George as the new duke, kindness will be bestowed upon everyone employed here."

"George, eh?" Mrs. Prowler said, placing a floury hand on her hip and making Vicky blush profusely. "Oh, don't worry about me, miss. Lord Warwick told me I could call him by his given name, too. Have you ever heard anything dafter in all your life? He may hold the title soon enough, but I'm not about ready to put myself in a pickle. It'll be his missus that'll run this house. I've no reason to worry, though, because Her Grace said I can stay here and work and I won't be forced to return to the London house."

"That was kind of her," Vicky said. "Did she tell you that good news today?"

"Oh, no," Mrs. Prowler said with a grunt as she turned the ball of dough over and dusted it with more flour. "That was last week." The sound of glass shattering down the hall had them both turning, and the cook breathed a curse under her breath. "If you'll excuse me, miss, I have to see who's ruining the crystal!" She bellowed the last as she walked past Vicky, clearly wanting whoever had broken something to know she was coming and that she was not happy with what she expected to find.

Vicky decided to go outside, but the rear gardens were out of the question if Lady Warwick and Richard were there doing whatever it was they were doing. Several images appeared in her mind, and she shivered.

Disgusting, she thought as she pushed them away in irritation.

As she walked through the main corridor that led to the front door, Vicky caught movement in the corner of her eye but when she looked, no one was there. She dismissed it. Her imagination had been running wild since arriving at this house!

Standing on the portico, she glanced about. A few dark clouds promised rain later in the day. At least she would be warm inside the grand house.

She descended the stairs and made her way to the stables in hopes of finding the constable there. Halfway to her destination, she caught sight of him leaning against an outbuilding just past the stables. He took a liberal swig from a flask and crumbs dotted his coat as she approached.

"Constable Cogwell? I have been looking for you."

"Oh," the constable replied as he pushed the flask into his inside pocket. "How may I assist you, Miss Parker?"

Vicky knew her next words had to be chosen carefully. She would need to direct the man toward George Warwick without outright accusing the marquess. It was one thing to believe him guilty and quite another to voice her suspicions. Plus, the duchess had given the man money to look elsewhere, which would be a difficulty she would have to overcome.

"I was just speaking to Lord Warwick," she said. "He is quite upset about the death of his father."

"As well he would be," the constable said, an air of arrogance to his tone. "His Grace was an exceptional man. Not that I knew him personally, of course, but from what his wife has told me, none could match his wit and intelligence."

Vicky forced a smile. "Indeed," she replied. "The trouble is, I had the distinct impression that Lord Warwick has information about the murder." When the constable frowned, she quickly added, "If he does know something, it would only help in your inquest, would it not?"

Several moments passed as the constable studied the ground between them. Would he outright refuse to hear what she had to say? If she could only lead this man to George, perhaps any guilt the marquess harbored would overtake him and lead him to confess to the murder.

Finally, Constable Cogwell replied, "Let us go speak to him, then. I do hope what you say is true. I certainly do not want to disturb a man of his importance unnecessarily."

"I truly believe what he knows will help you solve this crime."

"What makes you so certain?" the constable asked, leading her up the stairway to the front door of the house. "Did he say something specific to you?"

"Not necessarily," she replied. "But it is a feeling I have. Something is bothering him, that much I am sure. Perhaps he could use your wise counsel."

This made Constable Cogwell preen. "I have been known to give words of wisdom to those who need to hear them."

George still sat in his chair facing the window, just as she had left him.

"My lord," Vicky called, her heart thudding with anticipation at the man's upcoming confession. "The constable is here and wishes to speak with you."

However, there was no response.

"My lord?" Vicky repeated.

Nothing.

"George?"

The constable frowned. "Is he sleeping?" he asked. "Or perhaps he is praying. My grandfather would often doze off in the midst of the latter."

Curious, Vicky walked toward the desk. Then her eyes fell on a large candlestick lying on the floor beside him, and she hurried to his side.

"Constable!" she cried. Constable Cogwell joined her. "Is…is he dead?"

The form in the chair moaned. "Oh, my head," he mumbled, placing a hand on the back of his head as he sat upright. He looked up. "Vicky?" he asked. "Cogwell?"

"There now," the constable said. "Rest and do not move. It appears you were struck. Did you happen to see who hit you? What do you remember?"

"The last thing I remember was speaking with Miss Parker," the marquess replied, still rubbing his head. "I asked her to leave, but beyond that, I do not recall." To her surprise, he turned to Vicky. "Are you unharmed?" he asked with great concern. "You were not hurt, were you?"

Guilt tore through Vicky as a realization came to mind. Whoever the murderer was, it was not George Warwick. Her first instinct that he was too kind to kill his father had been correct. He had been nothing but hospitable to her, and her repayment was to summon the constable in a feeble attempt to gain a confession.

At least she had been careful with her words!

"No," she replied, "I am not hurt. I will leave the two of you alone."

With quick steps, Vicky moved out into the corridor and through the house to the rear gardens. Maybe it was time for her to return to London. She had no business playing constable here!

Chapter Twelve

The gray clouds that had been gathering in the distance now loomed above Vicky. She walked past the long row of hedges where a single bench sat looking over a large valley of green. At the bottom was a winding stream, its beginning and ending unknown.

Since no one was about, she dropped onto the bench like a child having a tantrum. She had nearly made a fool of herself believing George Warwick had murdered his father, and the sting of defeat did not sit well with her. She was not one to lose at anything to which she set her mind. So, why had she done so now?

The truth was abundantly clear. What business did she have running her own personal inquest into the death of the Duke of Everton? She was nothing more than a woman who managed the accounts of people who had enough money to use the services of a private accountant, something she herself could never afford. That and her ability to gossip with Laura Grant, the owner of the millinery in the shop beside hers. Neither gave her the credentials or training to do what Constable Cogwell did. Or rather what he was supposed to be doing.

A sense of sadness overtook her as she contemplated what to do next. If the constable made mention of her intentions, surely George would ask her to leave. She swallowed hard. No, not George but rather Lord Warwick. What right did she have to be considered a friend? A friend did not incriminate another friend for murder.

Regardless of how she addressed him, the marquess would insist she be sent away, as well as James, likely without pay and without need for further services.

"There you are."

She turned to find James approaching, but she did not rise to greet him. Instead, she dropped her chin into her hand and returned her unfixed gaze on the valley below.

"Did you hear?" James continued. "Lord Warwick was attacked in his study. It appears the murderer wants him dead, as well. So that begs the question, who would gain if both father and son were dead?"

"I did not need to hear," Vicky replied with a sigh. "It was Constable Cogwell and me who found him." She scowled. "After I convinced the constable to speak with Lord Warwick in order to get a confession out of him." Despair ran through her veins as she grasped her skirts in her fists. "I had the audacity to believe that the marquess killed his father. What a foolish notion! In my heart of hearts I knew he was not capable of murder, but I ran with it like a child running away from her mother with a handful of sweets!"

"Vicky, I would suggest—"

She did not wish to hear his justifications for her actions, for she did not deserve them. "How often have I been instructed to remain quiet, to allow others to complete the tasks assigned them, and to remain out of the way only to ignore such instruction? What I once dismissed as illogical and half-witted, I now see as wisdom. Yet, the lessons come far too late." Unshed tears stung her eyes. "Now, if you do not mind, I wish to return home today. You are welcome to remain if you wish, but I cannot face these people with this failure weighing on my shoulders. How will they see me once they learn of this betrayal to Lord Warwick?"

James heaved a sigh and lowered himself to a knee in front of her. Removing a handkerchief from his pocket, he offered it to her. "Do you remember the time you made stew?" he asked. "Two years ago, I believe it was. You had forgotten to add the carrots and became so upset about it, you nearly threw out the entire pot."

She nodded. "I do remember."

"What you are experiencing now is no different."

Vicky frowned. "I do not believe forgetting carrots in a stew and interfering with an inquest into murder can be judged the same."

James shook his head. "But they are the same in a way," he insisted. "Just as they are no different from when you considered closing your father's business."

Vicky's frown deepened and she leaped from the bench. "I have no idea what point you are attempting to make, but comparing Father's business to a stew is insulting! And to liken it to making an accusation for murder is even worse! One does not come close to the other in importance!"

"Forgive me," James said, his voice remaining calm in the harshness of her tone. "I meant no offense. What I am saying is this: all three examples are the same in that you experienced a great deal of doubt in each instance. You feared the stew would not be good enough, yet neither Percy nor I complained. As to your father's business, you feared you would be unable to run it yourself. Yet, look what you have done with it. The point is, you judge yourself much too quickly and there is no reason for it. Every challenge in life that has come your way, you have persevered and rose far above it."

Vicky sniffled. "But I had believed Lord Warwick—"

"And you were wrong. There is nothing wrong with being wrong."

"We are speaking of murder, not a stew."

"Be that as it may," James replied, "we all make mistakes. What makes a person different from others who err is what they decide to do next."

"What do you mean?"

"You may leave this very moment and return to London, or you may remain here and continue what you started. I will support either decision but let me say this. Do not allow fear to guide you. You are far better than that."

Dabbing at her eyes with the handkerchief, Vicky could not help but smile. A light breeze blew a loose strand of hair into her face, and James brushed it behind her ear.

"What have I done to deserve such a friend?" she asked. "You have always been the strength I have needed."

"I will not lie," James replied with a tiny smile, "my pride swells when you say such things, but the strength comes not from me but inside you. I am merely drawing your attention to it."

Overcome with joy, Vicky wrapped her arms around her friend. She always felt comfortable in his strong embrace. "What you say is true, and I cannot and will not feel pity for myself. I am a capable and intelligent woman — much more so than that idiotic constable. Therefore, I will learn who killed the duke before we leave for London tomorrow afternoon." She looked up and her heartbeat quickened, but she could not step away. "You will continue to help me, will you not?"

"Do you need to ask?"

Vicky knew she did not, for James had always been a dear friend, one who would never refuse any request she made.

And although it was likely inappropriate, she remained in his embrace, savoring the peace it brought her. For the first time in many years, she considered what he had said about fear. Fear was what made her swear to remain a spinster, to never test fate again. Yet, in the arms of James, she wondered if she should reconsider that notion.

**

With renewed vigor for finding the person who murdered the duke, Vicky returned to the great house, James at her side.

"Lord Warwick is in his study," James whispered. "I will go there to see what I can learn."

"Thank you," Vicky replied. She glanced up toward the staircase. The duchess had changed into a dark blue gown, her auburn hair neatly pinned into an elegant chignon. "While you do that, I will speak to someone who has not been telling me the truth."

Once James was gone, Vicky went to the bottom of the stairs and waited. Each step the duchess took, she let out a sigh, and at one point she stopped and placed a gloved hand to her forehead.

She had clearly seen Vicky waiting for her but seemed to enjoy the dramatics.

"My lady's maid informed me that George was attacked," she said. "Do you know if this is true?"

"Unfortunately, yes," Vicky replied. "He was in the study at the time but thankfully remains in good health."

The duchess clicked her tongue. "To think a killer is among us. Have you learned anything since we last spoke?"

Vicky glanced around to see if anyone was listening nearby. "I did, and what I learned may be of great interest to you. However, I would like to ask you a few questions if I may."

"Of course. I wish to find the murderer more than anyone here. Let us go to the library where we will not be interrupted." They proceeded to the library, the duchess's steps painfully slow. "I saw how much attention your blue dress drew," she said, "and chose one of the same color. Do you like it?"

"I do," Vicky replied. "I believe no lady in all of London could wear it better than you." In all honesty, she could not have cared less about this woman's gown, but flattery always produced the best results.

As they entered the library, the duchess went to the lounge and patted the seat beside her. "Come. Sit here where we can discuss your findings more intimately."

Vicky did as the woman bade, contemplating how she would broach the subject. Would it be best to come right out and say she knew of the affair the woman was having? Yet, if she did that, the accusation might seal the duchess's lips. No, she had to tread carefully.

"As you requested, I began my own inquest into your husband's death. Each person I interviewed revealed new information. Eventually, I was led to Lord Warwick."

"As I thought!" the duchess said. "He killed his father, just as I told you."

"That was the conclusion I made until he was attacked. This tells me it could not have been him."

The duchess adjusted the ring on her finger. "Could he not have struck himself in order to gain sympathy and deflect his guilt?"

"A wise thought, I am sure," Vicky said. "However, he was struck from behind." She frowned. "I can see your point, but would he go to such lengths to hide his guilt? It seems rather unlikely to me."

"I imagine that when one's life hangs in the balance, one will do whatever possible to keep all suspicion from him."

Vicky considered this for a moment. Would the duchess not also go to such lengths to hide her guilt, as well? "I suppose he could have set up the attack himself," she said with a shrug. "I will not ignore that point." She hesitated. "If I may, you spoke of Mr. Kent and how you would prefer he never return to your home."

Giving a look of disdain, the duchess replied, "Indeed. His ilk is no longer welcome in this house. Felton may have suffered his presence, but I certainly will not." Then she gasped. "Do you believe he could be responsible for my husband's death? It would not surprise me to learn that he is capable of murder."

"I am uncertain, to be honest," Vicky said. "However, he did allude to the possibility of you knowing more than you have admitted." She omitted the fact the man had made an outright accusation, once again knowing that saying so would put the woman on the defensive. If that were to happen, she would be left with no avenue for gaining any information.

"Richard Kent is a desperate man," the duchess replied. "Not only does he lust after me — oh, yes, my dear, I see the way he leers at me — but he is an incompetent fool who is jealous of what Felton and I had. You must understand, a woman with my beauty can drive any man to madness and cause him to insinuate the most unfathomable things. But to suggest that I killed Felton? What reason would I have to do that?"

Vicky knew that now was the time to strike, but it required a delicate hand. Or in this case, delicate words. "I could repeat what he said, but the notion is absurd and could never have a basis of truth. I fear it would offend you. Gossip and hearsay really cause more harm than good. Therefore, perhaps it would be best if I kept it to myself."

"Victoria, we are friends. Have I not said as much? Please, tell me, for I wish to know what others think of me. How will I ever improve if no one ever tells me?"

Giving an exaggerated sigh, Vicky replied, "He claims that you were not asleep as you stated but rather you were in this very room with..." She hesitated for dramatic effect. "With the baron."

"Me?" the duchess exclaimed. "Alone with William...erm...or rather with Lord Gerard? That is just plain silly. Why would I put myself in such a tenuous situation?"

"He maintains that it is because you believed that if you helped Lord Gerard secure a deal with the duke, you could find a way to keep this house." Vicky dropped her gaze to the floor as if embarrassed to say what followed. "Thus securing a future for you and the baron. Together." She glanced up through her eyelashes to gauge the other woman's reaction.

The duchess's shoulders slumped. "I never loved Felton," she whispered. "I had turned eighteen only days before my father announced that I was to be married. Before I knew it, the banns were read, and I found myself here as a new bride. For most young ladies, it would have been a dream come true, but I had other aspirations for myself. Yes, I married well, but I wished to marry for love."

She sniffled and wiped her nose on a handkerchief she pulled from the bodice of her gown. "Then I met William. I had not intended to hurt my husband, but he made it clear he could never love me. Why he wished to marry me had never been made clear. I could not even be the mother of his heir, for his former wife had already borne his first son. It was not long before I realized that I was nothing more than entertainment to relieve his boredom on cold nights. Even a maid could have fulfilled that need."

"You found peace in the arms of the baron," Vicky said quietly. "I take it you made plans to live together?"

The duchess nodded. "When the duke announced at the party that we would be relocating to India, I already knew, for I overheard him telling a friend nearly a month ago. The idea of living so far from William tore me apart, so I decided to ask Felton if I could remain here for a short time and join him later."

"But you had no intention of joining him, am I correct in saying so?"

She nodded again. "When I made my request, he refused, and no amount of groveling and explaining could sway his decision once he made it. Because my appointment came after William's, we planned to meet here so I could give him Felton's response."

"And what about the constable?" Vicky asked. "Did you pay him off to steer the inquest away from you as a possible suspect?"

"Not for the reason you may believe," the duchess replied firmly. "I feared that Constable Cogwell would learn of my affair with William and use that as a reason to implicate me. Or William, for that matter. I could not have him nosing into matters that would lead to terrible rumors about me, even if they were true. Please, I hope you will keep the particulars of my relationship with William to yourself and that you do not think ill of me."

"I do not judge you for what you have done," Vicky replied. "And I will keep your affair private, but I must ask you one last question. I hope you will trust me enough to answer truthfully."

"Of course. You may ask me anything."

"Did you kill your husband?"

The duchess did not hesitate in her reply. "No. I would never entertain such a thought. I admit that I wished the man would fall asleep and never wake, but I can assure you that I would never take the life of another person, including my husband. Even for love."

"And the baron? Would he commit murder so the two of you could be together?"

"I would say the same about him. William would never hurt anyone. He may seem a bear, but he has the heart of a lamb." She giggled. "But do not tell him I said so. He would be mortified if he learned I compared him to a lamb."

"I will keep that tidbit to myself," Vicky said, although she doubted the woman's opinion of the baron. "There is one problem with your assessment, however. Your husband was poisoned, and you had the baron give him a decanter of brandy. It does not bode well for him. Or you."

A look of confusion crossed the duchess's face. "But William did not give Felton the brandy. It was George. I saw him myself come and retrieve the decanter from right over there." She pointed to a cabinet beside the door.

"You were here when he took it?"

"William and I both were, but William hid behind the drapes so he would not be seen alone with me."

Vicky was uncertain what to think of this new information. All evidence pointed to Lord Warwick, but the fact he had been attacked from behind and nearly died from that blow removed the culpability from him. Then an obvious question came to mind.

"Why was the brandy stored here of all places?"

The duchess laughed. "George is like a child. He did not want his father to stumble across his gift, so he asked Richard to hide it here during dinner last evening."

Vicky could not stop her eyes from widening. Richard had left the table in the middle of dinner the night before, which placed him alone with the very decanter that held the brandy that had killed the duke. That begged the question, had it been he who poisoned the brandy?

Vicky was determined to learn the truth, that much was certain!

Chapter Thirteen

It was two hours before dinner would be served, which gave Vicky time to search out Richard before changing. Voices rose from behind the closed sitting room doors, and she stopped to listen, straining to see if she could make out the voice of Richard. He would be easy to distinguish, even in the lower tones, for he was an obnoxious man who would certainly offer his unwanted opinion at any given moment.

Her patience ran thin when she could not identify either voice, so she made her way upstairs. Perhaps she would wait until after dinner, where she could pull him aside to question him.

As she passed the room assigned to him, however, she stopped and listened. If he was in his room at this very moment, would now not be a prudent time to speak with him?

Just as she went to knock, a woman's voice came to her ear. What was Lady Warwick doing in Richard's private room?

"I am not certain I believe you," the marchioness said in simpering tones. "There are so few I can trust, and even if I did trust you, I doubt you would be able to manage to pull it off."

Vicky frowned. Were they discussing a celebration for Lord Warwick's birthday as the marquess had said? If so, why would they do so in such an intimate location?

"Then remain here with your husband." That voice clearly belonged to Richard. "After all, he will soon be named as the new Duke of Everton and you his duchess. He will be so busy in his new role that getting rid of him will prove impossible."

Vicky covered her mouth in shock. They could only be plotting one thing — the death of Lord Warwick!

"Tell me now, Lavinia, for I grow tired of waiting."

Lady Warwick sighed heavily. "I have no choice, I suppose. If you can encourage the man to follow in his father's footsteps, I will reward you greatly."

"How?" Richard demanded. "Money? Land?"

"What we shared in the garden today is but a taste of what you will receive," Lady Warwick replied, the simpering returned. "Now, I must return to my husband, but if I learn that it was you who struck him, the deal is off."

Richard laughed. "You do not mean that."

"Do I not?" All simpering was now gone. "Do not test me!"

Hearing footsteps, Vicky scurried away to her own room. With her back against the closed door, she willed her racing heart to calm. Had it been Richard who struck Lord Warwick after all? If so, had he also murdered the duke? And what did Lady Warwick mean about her husband following the same path as his father?

Vicky counted to ten, drew in a deep breath, and cracked the door open only to come face to face with Richard. With a great yelp, she drew back and slammed the door closed. When Richard knocked, she opened the door once more, this time with purpose.

"What do you want?" she demanded.

"Hello, Victoria," Richard said with a mischievous grin. "Does my handsomeness frighten you in some way?"

The impertinence of this man knew no bounds!

Vicky raised her chin defiantly. "Your mere presence brings back memories of falling ill after a winter storm when I was a child."

"I wish to speak with you," he said, undaunted. "May I come in?"

She glanced over her shoulder. "Do not be silly," she replied. "Why would I allow you to be alone with me in my room?"

"You make a good point," he said, rubbing his chin. "But you have no qualms about being alone with me in my room, so let us go there." He turned as if expecting her to follow.

"Come back here this instance," she shouted after him.

Much to her chagrin, he ignored her and entered his room, leaving the door open behind him.

She hurried down the corridor and peeked into the room. "I refuse to be caught in your room alone again, Mr. Kent."

Richard waved a dismissive hand at her. "Everyone else is with Warwick in the sitting room," he replied. "No one will know. I have important matters to discuss with you concerning the death of the duke."

Vicky considered her options. If Richard was indeed the murderer, which was becoming more evident, entering his room alone was a fool's errand. Yet, she also recognized that being murdered in his room would make it clear who had been the murderer all along. The question was, was she willing to make that sacrifice?

Making a quick decision, she closed the door behind her and said, "Do not think that me entering your room gives you permission to any acts of lewdness. If I have the slightest inkling you will be inappropriate in any way, I will scream. Is that clear?" She refused to walk further into the room. Instead, she kept her hand on the door's handle in case she needed to make a quick getaway.

Richard chuckled as he walked over to the window. "Now, darling—"

"I do not respond to darling or any other pet names," she snapped. "Please refrain from using them with me."

"You take all the fun out of everything," he said in mock dolefulness as he continued to stare out the window. "Victoria," he said her name with emphasis, "do you believe the duchess murdered her husband?"

"No, I do not," she replied, staring at Richard's back. He was such a rude man! "Or at least I do not think her the most likely to have murdered him."

"Then who do you believe is the culprit?"

"I am not exactly certain as of yet. Who do you believe it may have been?"

"I, too, am unsure, but George Warwick remains high on my list." He turned to face her. "You say you are uncertain, but you must have a hypothesis."

She gave a nervous laugh. "I doubt you wish to hear who I suspect," she replied.

"Let me be the judge of that."

"In that case, let me say that I believe I may be close. Whoever killed the duke also went after his son. Rumors abound that you and Lady Warwick are having an affair and therefore, I would guess that it was you. Unless you can convince me otherwise."

To this, Richard threw back his head and laughed. "I am having an affair with Lady Warwick?" he asked. "Whose asinine idea was that?" He blanched. "My apologies for my crude language, but you can understand how upsetting such talk can be."

"I heard the two of you speaking," Vicky said.

He frowned. "When?"

"Just before you came to my room. I overheard the two of you planning to get rid of George!"

He frowned. "That is what she wants me to do, but not in the way you think. She wants him sent away to India in his father's place." He strode over to glare down at her. "But no one is to know about that."

Pressing her back into the door, she managed to squeak, "If you try to kill me, I shall scream. And even if I am unable to scream, my body will be found in your room. Either way, everyone will learn it was you who took the duke's life!"

"You are far too dramatic for your own good," Richard replied, with a deep chuckle. "I have never taken the life of another person, nor do I plan to do so anytime soon."

He turned and walked over to a table with two chairs beside it. "Would you like me to explain what Lavinia...Lady Warwick and I are planning?" he asked as he held out a hand indicating one of the chairs.

Vicky stared at him. She had no intention of leaving her place by the door. "Yes, please explain."

He sighed when she refused to sit. "When Lady Warwick learned the duke was planning to leave for India, she asked me to convince him to allow George to join him. Of course, His Grace refused. I thought the matter over until today."

"What happened today?"

"The marchioness asked me to accompany her on a stroll through the gardens, where she proposed a new plan. I was to encourage George to take the journey in his father's place. To book passage to India and spend at least a year there as a way to honor the duke's memory."

"And Lady Warwick would remain here alone," Vicky murmured.

"Exactly. According to her, she needs time to be alone or some other rubbish."

"And you were willing to convince the marquess of this?" Vicky asked. She snorted. "Of course you would. You and the marchioness are quite friendly, are you not? As in the romantic sense."

The look of affront he gave her nearly made her laugh. "I have never been more offended in my life! Why would you think so poorly of me?"

"It is not that difficult," she replied. "I can only assume that the rumors about your roguish ways are true. Therefore, not only did the two of you kiss today in the garden, I suspect you did so last night, as well." When Richard slumped in his chair, Vicky knew she had cornered him, caught him in his own lies. "Oh, yes, I know you were alone with her last night. Do not deny it!"

Richard leaped from his chair and reached inside his coat. "It is not what you think. This is what she gave me today in the garden." He slammed a wad of notes onto the table. "And she promised me more."

"And last night?" Vicky asked. "Why were you alone with her then?"

Richard sighed. "It was shortly after dinner. We were alone no more than two minutes when she mentioned her husband's upcoming birthday. We met today to plan a party for him."

Likely excuse, Vicky thought. Aloud she said, "And the bottle of brandy? You hid it away in the library for Lord Warwick to collect later. Is that not true?"

"Yes, but—"

"Then you could have easily poisoned it to make it appear that Lord Warwick killed his father." For a moment, she thought he would not respond. Or that he would strike her.

Yet, he did neither. Instead, he smirked. "Very good, Victoria," he said, clapping his hands together in mock applause. "There is one problem with your theory, however. What motive would I have for killing the duke?" He gave her no opportunity to reply and answered for her. "You see? There is none. And although it was I who hid the brandy in the library, it was not at the request of George, nor that of Lavinia, but rather of Gerard."

Vicky's eyes widened. "The baron? But that cannot be. He was to meet the duchess in the library. Why have you hide it if he was planning to go there anyway?"

"I have asked myself the same thing all day. All I know is that he asked me to hide it during dinner, and I was paid handsomely to do so."

Vicky searched his eyes for any sign of deceit, but much to her frustration, she found none.

Richard grinned. "I recognize that look," he said, taking a step toward her. "It is one of desire. Allow me to kiss you in order to quench the fire that burns inside you."

With a sheepish smile, she replied, "Close your eyes."

When his eyes were shut, she opened the door and slipped into the corridor, where she drew in heavy breaths. The man was definitely a scoundrel, a rogue, a womanizer. But a killer? Unlikely.

Chapter Fourteen

Vicky hurried to the dining room, her skirts swishing around her ankles in her haste. Her heart pounded. Would the others be angry for her tardiness?

As she neared the room, the low murmur of voices came to her ear as she slowed her step. The frowns that greeted her when she entered told her that, indeed, some were not pleased they had been forced to wait for dinner to be served.

Several chairs scraped the floor as the men stood, but it was James who came to her rescue.

"Are you feeling better, Miss Parker?" he asked. Then he addressed the party. "Her worries over what happened to Lord Warwick made her feel unwell, you see. She had been with the constable when he was found, after all."

"I am better, thank you," she replied. She grasped her skirts and dropped into a deep curtsy. "My apologies for my tardiness, my lord."

The marquess tutted and waved her to her feet. "None of us will die of hunger if you are a few minutes late," he said with a kind smile. "I am glad someone has shown concern for my health on this dreary evening." Lady Warwick gave a tiny gasp of annoyance, and her husband quickly added, "I meant that I am pleased with the show of concern I have received from everyone. Please, Miss Parker, we are ready to begin."

No sooner had Vicky sat than Richard entered the room. "My apologies," he said with a bow. "I find it comforting to read a few lines of scripture before I eat and found myself lost in the Good Book."

Several people nodded in approval, but Vicky rolled her eyes. She doubted rather highly Richard had come within a hundred feet of a church or even glanced at a Bible. He was much too disagreeable for such pastimes.

Then a terrible thought came to her. They both had been late to dinner, one arriving only moments before the other. Would there now be rumors that she and Richard were in some sort of romantic entanglement? Yet, there were no sudden hushed whispers behind hands or suspicious glances in either of their direction. Thank heavens!

A line of footmen entered to place bowls of steaming pea soup before each guest. Spoons clinked on bowls as everyone began to eat, but a sudden clank had everyone turn to stare at Lady Warwick.

"Take this away," she demanded of the footman assigned to her. "And you tell Mrs. Prowler that I will speak to her — again, mind you — about how much mint she puts in the soup. If I have told her once, I have told her a thousand times, I do not like mint!" She said the last with punctuated stress on each word.

"I think it is lovely," Lord Warwick said. "The mint gives it a wonderful—"

Vicky had to agree with Lord Warwick. The soup was lovely.

Lady Warwick sniffed, however. "If my opinion holds no bearing now, how will the staff ever see me as their new mistress when the time arises, George?" she demanded.

The marquess sighed. "Serve the next course," he said to the head footman, who took his bowl with a bow. The others collected the remaining bowls and followed him out the hidden servants' door in a far corner.

"I understand you wish to take your rightful place as duchess, my dear," the duchess said, "but upsetting Mrs. Prowler will not get you there. May I make a suggestion?"

Lady Warwick pursed her lips and lifted her glass of wine with meticulous movements. "If you believe you should." It was clear she had no desire to hear anything the other woman had to say, but what could one do in front of a roomful of guests?

"Put in a request — kindly, mind you — to have a separate portion made up for you that does not contain mint. Thus, Mrs. Prowler is given the opportunity to show her abilities but also meets your expectations at the same time. You both win."

The marchioness glanced around the table. "I appreciate your kind counsel, Your Grace," she said, acid in her tone despite the smile on her face. "I will take your words to advisement."

The next course arrived without incident, and as everyone ate, Vicky looked over each guest once more in an attempt to determine who could have killed the duke and attacked the marquess. The duchess had the greatest motive but she lacked the opportunity. Lady Warwick wished to be away from her husband, but she did not wish to see him hurt.

The baron, however, was a man so self-absorbed that he was still inspecting his fork. "I am quite impressed at how well-polished your silver is," he said, twisting the utensil in his fingers. "Your butler must show mine how polishing is done properly."

"I am sure Sheplin will be pleased by your compliment," Lord Warwick replied. "He has been in our family for years."

As the men continued a discussion of their expectations for staff, Vicky's mind drifted away once more. In fact, her mind was so far away that when she looked back down at her plate, it was a different dish altogether. The fricassee of chicken and mushrooms was wonderful, and she savored every bite. She would miss eating so well when they returned home.

When Vicky glanced up at the duchess, the woman gave her a warm smile. Vicky could not imagine being married to a man so much her elder as the duchess had, but it was not all that uncommon. A father would offer anything to see his daughter marry a duke.

"Miss Parker," Lord Warwick said, snapping her out of her thoughts, "are you enjoying the wine?"

For a moment, all Vicky could do was stare at the marquess. She knew her face had to be ten shades of red. Why would he be interested in her opinion about the wine? What she drank at home would never grace even the servants' table here!

"Oh, yes," she replied. "It is very nice. I have never tasted anything so bold." What it meant when one said wine was bold was beyond her, but she had heard others of better means describe wines as such, so that was the term she used.

"I could not agree with you more," Lord Warwick replied with a smile. "I selected it myself. This is the first time I have been allowed to do such a thing, for father always made these types of decisions." He glanced around the table. "Which I imagine comes as a surprise to many of you. That I am capable of making decisions." His tone held a bitterness to it that puckered more than one person's face.

Then she realized everyone was staring at her! Did they expect a response? Panic overtook her, and she prayed no mention of elephants left her lips.

"You are quite wise, my lord," she said, pleased her voice did not quake when her leg was bouncing beneath the table. "Quite capable in anything to which you put your mind." Everyone continued to stare, and before she could stop herself, she added, "That is all."

Lady Warwick frowned, and the baron smirked. All Vicky wanted to do was drop to the floor out of everyone's sight and crawl out of the room. Once again, they must have thought her a complete imbecilic.

The marquess, however, smiled. "Thank you for saying so. Your words bring me peace in these dark times."

And to Vicky's surprise, the duchess added, "I could not agree more. They stirred my heart, as well, for although she said the words to you, they brought to mind my beloved husband." Then she gasped and dropped her fork. "Oh, forgive me! It was not my intention to ruin such a lovely meal with my grief."

"Why is it that when my husband receives praise," Lady Warwick retorted, "you make a spectacle of yourself?" She then gasped as she pushed back her chair and stood, pressing a hand to her breast with dramatic flair. Several chairs scraped the floor as the men stood. "Forgive me, my friends, for my outburst. I have no idea what has come over me. It is a sudden bout of madness I cannot explain."

Lord Warwick hurried to his wife's side. "My love, please sit." He helped her back into her chair and handed her a glass of wine. "We are all under a great deal of stress, but our constable will soon learn who has been plotting the treachery that invades our home. I have complete and utter confidence in his capabilities."

Vicky stifled a snort as the guests resumed their meals as if none of the theatrics had taken place. She could not help but wonder if all titled families argued as much as the Warwicks in the presence of company. If so, how did they conduct themselves in private? She could not even imagine the rows that took place when no one was there to witness their behavior.

The truth was, most people wore a mask to conceal their idiosyncrasies, but Vicky had no doubt whatsoever that one person at this table went well beyond what was typical. For that person had committed murder.

By the time the final course was served, Vicky wondered how she could eat another morsel. Yet, the red currant tart looked all too appetizing to refuse. As they ate, the marquess regaled the party with a story about an outing with his wife after they had first married.

"So, of course, I handed over the money," Lord Warwick was saying about a business venture that had fallen into his lap, "for what person in his right mind would refuse such an offer?" Several people chuckled politely in response.

"George, you are slouching," Lady Warwick admonished in a low hiss that was loud enough for the entire party to hear.

The marquess shifted in his seat, his smile gone once again.

His wife gave a firm nod and grabbed her wine glass once more.

Vicky had lost count of how much wine the marchioness had consumed thus far.

"What my husband fails to mention is that because a contract was not drawn up, nothing came of it. We learned later that the man had no land or the castle he so eloquently insisted he owned, and we never saw him again." She heaved a heavy sigh. "That is why it is I who will be tasked with the responsibility of seeing this house is run correctly." As if an afterthought, she turned to the marquess and said in a sweet voice, "My husband knows I am willing to take on such responsibilities because I care for him."

"Yes, I do, my love," Lord Warwick replied. "And I am thankful for that."

Hurried footsteps in the hall made everyone turn as the constable entered the room unannounced and gasping for breath.

"George," Lady Warwick said with a frown, "why is that man in our dining room? Shall we allow the dogs in next?"

Lord Warwick rose. "Cogwell, what is the meaning of this interruption?"

"Forgive me, my lord, but I came to inform you that I found the man responsible for your father's death. Please, everyone, come with me."

***

"This is madness," Vicky whispered to James as they made their way down the long corridor. "How on earth did this man figure it out before us?"

"I am unsure," James replied. "But I admit I am curious to see whom he believes it is."

They followed the others to the study, and the constable made his way to the desk, where he waited until everyone gathered around him.

"I pray this does not take long," the baron growled. "I was looking forward to an after-dinner glass of port."

"What have you learned, Cogwell?" Lord Warwick asked.

The constable let out a dramatic sigh that lasted longer than most songs Vicky had heard. "My inquiry led me to investigate those within your home rather than without. I realized that the murderer had to have the capability of moving about the house without drawing suspicion. Because of this, every person within the home is a suspect."

The baron yawned. Richard whispered in the ear of Lady Warwick, who giggled.

What could those two be discussing? Vicky wondered, but before she could consider it further, the constable continued.

"However, when you were struck, my lord, I knew I had to propel my inquest, for the murderer is becoming more brazen and I feared he would strike again. Such is the desire of a madman, to continue to hunt those he despises as if they were some sort of prey. It is much like what we see in nature, the wild beast attacking those around them in an attempt to—"

"Constable," Lady Warwick snapped, "you insult me by entering the dining room while we are eating, and now you insult my intelligence with this idiotic speech. Please, get to the point of this meeting."

Constable Cogwell cleared his throat. "Yes, of course." He reached into his coat and produced a brass candlestick. "This is the very weapon used to strike the marquess. Do you notice anything about it, my lord?"

The marquess studied it. "It is one of many," he replied with a shrug. "They are all over the house."

"But this went missing," the constable said with a grin. "And I know where it came from."

Vicky felt a mixture of emotion as Constable Cogwell spoke. On one hand, she was pleased the constable had found the murderer, thus making them all safe once more. On the other hand, she was disappointed that she had failed at finding the killer herself.

"You see, earlier I encountered your butler, Sheplin, polishing several of these exact same candlesticks." He glanced around, his grin widening, but then his smile dropped. "Again, I say that they were exactly like this one."

"What?" the baron asked as he shook his head. "Do you expect applause?"

"I am afraid I do not understand," the duchess said, frowning. "What is the importance of all this?"

Then a voice from behind them made everyone turn. "I can tell you what he is implying," Sheplin said as he entered the room. "Since I was polishing the other candlesticks, I must be the culprit in Lord Warwick's assault. Apparently, I am the only person here capable of picking up such an object and no one else."

The constable's grin widened further. "Is that your confession, then?" he demanded.

Sheplin shook his head. "I confess to cleaning the candlesticks, but nothing more. This man's accusation is absurd, my lord. Why would I want to harm you or wish His Grace dead?"

Lord Warwick turned to the constable. "Sheplin has been with my family for years," he said. "I can assure you he would not harm me or my father."

Lady Warwick, however, took a step forward, her face pensive. "Do not be so quick to dismiss him," she said. "Perhaps it was he who committed these horrible crimes."

"But my love—"

"Tell me, Sheplin," the marchioness said, ignoring her husband, "were you not angry that His Grace was leaving Stanting Estate and planned to leave you behind? He did not invite you to accompany him to India, did he?"

"It is not my place--," the butler stammered, but Lady Warwick would hear none of it.

"It was you who struck my husband and poisoned my father-in-law," she gasped. "How could you betray us so?"

"If I have completed my inquest," Constable Cogwell said, "may I have my dinner? I have yet to eat, and I am—"

"You will eat when I say," Lady Warwick snapped. "I wish for a response from the butler. An honest response, mind you. Tell me, do you wish harm on my husband?"

Sheplin closed his eyes, and Vicky stifled a gasp. Surely he did not kill the duke! And she was sure he would not harm a hair on the marquess's head. Of all the people she suspected of either act, he was very low on the list.

The butler opened his eyes and smiled. "I have no desire to harm anyone, least of all my employers. Now, do you wish to review this week's order for food and drink, or should the good constable deliver me to the jail?" Although he stood tall and proud, there was a tone of frustration in his voice. Vicky did not blame him.

"You may return to your duties," Lord Warwick said kindly. "Why not ready the sitting room for after-dinner drinks?"

"What are you doing?" his wife demanded.

"You know as well as I, Lavinia, that this man did nothing wrong." He turned to the rest of the party. "Please, let us retire to the sitting room."

As the guests filed out of the study, Vicky overheard the marchioness admonishing her husband. "It is so like you to not wish to find the malefactor!"

Once they were in the corridor, James whispered to Vicky, "I believe the constable is growing desperate. We must find the murderer before he points fingers at us!"

"That is just plain silly," she said. "Why would he suddenly decide we are guilty? We have the least amount of motive." She snorted. "I am beginning to wonder if he will bother to include any of the guests in his inquiry." She glanced over her shoulder to find the constable standing in the doorway of the study, glaring at their backs. "You know, you may be right after all," she said, lowering her voice further. "We must hurry if we are to keep him from charging us with murder!"

Chapter Fifteen

As the port and sherry flowed, the tension between Lady Warwick and the duchess seemed to ease. In fact, the mood of the entire party improved tremendously, no doubt brought on by the drink they consumed.

"It appears the rain will continue throughout the night," Lord Warwick said, gaining everyone's attention as he stood. "But it does not matter, for I say we go to the ballroom and enjoy the finest music ever heard. Come, my friends, for it is time I revealed my surprise."

Vicky rose and followed the party as they made their way toward the ballroom, but she was forced to grit her teeth when the baron stepped in front of her as if she were not there. He made no attempts to apologize to rectify his rudeness, but when he turned in the doorway, she realized his rudeness had a purpose.

"Miss Parker, I wish to speak with you." Without waiting for her reply, he closed the door, leaving them alone in the sitting room. "Let us sit so we are more comfortable."

Vicky glanced at the door. "I mean no disrespect, my lord, but I must admit that being alone with you is making me uncomfortable. Please allow me to pass so I may enjoy the festivities with the others."

Lord Gerard raised a single eyebrow. "I believe you will find it worth your while," he said. "And I insist you remain."

His voice brooked no argument, and a shiver of fright ran down Vicky's back. Yet, she summoned her courage and reached for the door handle behind the baron. To her surprise, he grasped her wrist with a firm grip.

"I know about Duncan Blackmoore."

Vicky froze in place. "I have no idea of whom you speak, my lord," she lied. "Now, allow me to pass."

"You are lying to me," the baron replied. "I met the man a few months ago, and he told me all about your sordid affair as well as how you became a spinster."

Painful memories filled Vicky's mind. A field of green, a picnic basket, and a bottle of wine. There Duncan confessed his love for her, promising that he had no interest in any other. She had thought herself the luckiest woman in the world.

"He also mentioned the revenge you sought on his estate," Lord Gerard continued. "Tell me, Miss Parker, did you set fire to his home to spite him? You were lucky no lives were lost, but many valuables were."

Vicky pulled her wrist from his grasp. "I know no Duncan Blackmoore, as I said, but I can assure you that if I did, I would not have been anywhere near his home." The latter was the truth, for although Duncan had broken her heart and she was angry, she would never do anything to harm him or his property in any way.

Word had arrived concerning the country cottage belonging to Duncan, the very place where her heartbreak had happened. She may have wished to delete him from her life, but that did not mean she was willing to wipe him from the face of the earth.

"Blackmoore is a much better man than I," the baron said, "for I would have seen you thrown into prison for your crimes as soon as I learned you were responsible for them. I could inform the constable this very moment, in fact. Of course, rumor would travel through London, and every client you possess would distance themselves from you."

"Why do you threaten me?" Vicky demanded. "We have never been acquainted until this weekend!" Tears stung her eyes. Her father had begun his accounting business with only a single client, a butcher, and had grown it into the profitable firm it was today. So, why did this man wish to bring it down?

"Charlotte told me what you found out about us," Lord Gerard said in a deep growl. "I must know that our affair will be kept secret, at least for now. There is too much at stake. Not only do we have a great affection for one another, but I also want to see success in the business I wish to conduct with the new Duke of Everton."

Vicky raised herself to her full height, which still did not reach the baron's shoulder. "Unlike you, I do not engage in gossip. Nor do I threaten others. You may hold the title of baron, but I have seen servants show more respect than you could ever earn. I will keep what I know to myself, not because of your threats but rather because I wish to protect Her Grace, who is worthy of my respect."

"That is all I needed to hear," the baron replied as he opened the door and stepped aside. Then he used an arm to bar her exit. "But know this. I never make idle threats. Therefore, if you cannot keep your end of this bargain, I will rain down so much trouble, you will be unable to survive it."

For a moment, only the sound of the pelting rain on the window and distant rumble of thunder was all Vicky could hear. She considered what James had told her earlier, that she had a strength inside her that allowed her to overcome any obstacle. Would that strength see her through what this man could do to her? Did he control her fate?

No! She would not allow it!

As if a candlewick had been lit inside her, she raised her chin and replied, "You should also not forget that the duchess considers me a friend," she snapped. "As does the marquess. If I were to approach them—"

"You dare threaten me?"

"I make no threats, my lord," she replied as she stepped past him.

"However, I will say this. If any rumor does happen to come to my ears concerning my past, another will leave my lips. And I speak of more than your affair."

Lord Gerard chuckled. "You have nothing with which to blackmail me," he said with a smug grin. "I will call your bluff."

"Is that so?" Vicky asked. "The bottle of brandy the duke drank last evening? I understand that it was left in your care. And I am not the only person who is aware of this fact. Two others know. What would people think if they learned you plan to marry a dowager duchess, whose husband was murdered, and that you handled the very drink the duke consumed?"

The baron's grin dropped, replaced by alarm. "That may be true," he blustered, "but it is not as it seems!" His panic was clear now. "To be told — told, mind you! — to deliver the brandy like some common servant! I am far better than that, which is why I asked that fool Kent to do it instead. I paid him rather handsomely for it, too! Therefore, you can see that I never placed a finger on that decanter!"

"Perhaps you are telling the truth," Vicky mused. "However, the duke is now dead, your business with Lord Warwick is now in the works, and you and the widow stand to gain a great deal of wealth. I may go and speak to Lord Warwick and tell him what I know."

"No!" Lord Gerard cried. "I beg of you, do not tell him! I am innocent of any wrongdoing, at least in the sense of murder!"

"If I were to believe you — and trust me, I am finding it quite difficult to do so — then who do you believe murdered the duke and why?" She narrowed her eyes. "Are you protecting the duchess, perhaps?" The baron shook his head. "Then who?"

"I wish I knew," he replied. "Warwick — the father, not the son — we argued from time to time, but we never reached a point where I would even consider taking his life. You must believe me!"

"If you wish me to accept your defense, then you must tell me everything you did last night."

The baron sighed. "I was with Charlotte in the library when the duke was killed. When I heard Richard summon the butler, I sneaked back to my room. That was when I saw…" He pulled at the bottom hem of his coat.

"What?" Vicky demanded. "What did you see?"

Lord Gerard swallowed visibly. "Lady Warwick. I saw her returning to her rooms, and I am certain it was well past the hour of her appointment."

***

With confident steps, Vicky made her way to the ballroom. Music from a variety of stringed instruments met her as she entered the room, and she came to an overwhelmed stop at the door.

No words could describe the sheer magnitude and luxury of the ballroom. The panels on the wall had been painted gold with white frames. Scarlet velvet curtains hung from floor to ceiling in front of large windows and sets of double doors that led out to the rear gardens. It all seemed much too grand for such a small party, but Vicky had seen the amount those of the *ton* were willing to spend even for intimate gatherings. Oftentimes it was enough to pay the rent for every shop on her street for several years!

"Excuse me."

Vicky turned to find Constable Cogwell trying to get past her. Why he did not simply go around was beyond her, for the door was wide enough to allow ten men standing side by side to pass through at once.

"I am needed," the constable continued, as if he had to explain his comings and goings to the likes of her. "You may watch if you wish."

"May I have your attention, please," Lady Warwick said, raising her voice to be heard above the music. "George, please tell those buffoons to stop playing for a moment."

Lord Warwick did as his wife bade, and the room fell silent.

"Thank you. If you will all join me here, I would like to make an important announcement."

Once everyone was gathered around a long table that held a bowl filled with punch, several bottles of wine, and lines of glasses, the marchioness continued.

"I have several varieties of our finest wines available for everyone's enjoyment. I believe it only fair that the constable taste each one to see that it meets his approval."

Vicky had never heard anything so ludicrous, but she had attended too few social functions of this caliber to know for certain. However, judging by the shocked looks of the others, this was not common.

Lady Warwick motioned to a nearby footman, who poured a small amount of each type of wine into several glasses. Vicky glanced around her and was relieved to see her confusion mirrored on the faces of the other guests.

The constable was outright beaming. "It is an honor to be the taster of such fine vintages," he said, choosing the closest glass to him and lifting it to peer through it. "One would not guess that I—"

"Oh, do stop your blustering," the baron grumbled. "The rest of us would like to drink, too, you know."

Constable Cogwell swished the wine around in the glass, sniffed it, and then took a tiny sip. One would have thought he did this more often than he probably had. "This is quite good," he said. "It may be the best I have ever tasted."

Richard, who stood beside Vicky, leaned in and whispered, "The woman is crafty. The fool believes he is being honored when in fact he is being used."

"Used?" Vicky asked. "How so?" Then she gasped. "You think she is using him to test if the wine is poisoned?"

Richard did not reply, but his look told her that was exactly what he thought. Vicky found the idea outright appalling! What would the marchioness do if the man did indeed encounter poison in one of the wines and died because of it?

The constable moved from glass to glass until he sipped from the last, declaring them all to the best he had ever had.

With a wide smile, Lady Warwick said, "Thank you for your time, constable, and good evening to you."

Constable Cogwell's smile dropped. "But I thought—"

"Hurry along now," the marchioness said, waving him away with a hand. As he made his way toward the door, she motioned to the musicians. "Now that civility has returned, let us enjoy the evening!"

At once, the guests scattered, some off to dance while others chose drinks. Lady Warwick turned to Vicky and clicked her tongue. "I cannot believe that man thought he could remain here with us. I would never allow a party to distract him from his inquest. If you will excuse me, I must speak to my husband. I fear he may be talking about business already, and I would like our guests to have an enjoyable evening." She hurried away, leaving Vicky standing alone.

Noticing James standing in front of one of the great windows, Vicky joined him.

"I never paid much attention to the sound of rain on a window before," James said. "I had always thought it more a nuisance, but for the first time I hear its melody." He laughed. "I must sound quite mad speaking of rain as musical."

"Not at all," Vicky replied, turning her gaze to the gardens beyond, appearing warped through the water that ran down the panes. "Have you been enjoying yourself?"

"I have," James said. "Lord Warwick asked my advice. He is thinking of leaving for India. Apparently, Mr. Kent has suggested he go and complete the journey his father was unable to take."

"And what advice did you give him?" Vicky asked.

"I told him he should do whatever he wishes to do and nothing more." He turned toward Vicky. "I must admit, I did feel a bit guilty for speaking to him."

"Why? You did nothing wrong. He asked for your opinion and you gave it."

James sighed. "In the sitting room was a small vase that looked so enticing, I could not help but steal it. I hid it in my room and plan to bring it home with us. It is for you, of course."

For a moment, Vicky could only stare at him before she saw the corners of his mouth begin to twitch. He was teasing her! "Well, the next time we receive an invitation," she said, "I will be sure to leave you at the office to work. We certainly cannot have you donned with the reputation that you are nothing more than a thief and cannot be trusted."

He gasped in mock surprise. "You would not do such a thing to me, would you?"

"No, of course not," she replied, still smiling. "I could not imagine being anywhere without you."

She clamped her mouth shut. Her cheeks burned and her legs felt a tad wobbly. What had compelled her to make such an absurd statement, even in jest?

James made no comment as he turned his gaze back to the window, his damaged hand behind his back.

"I spoke to the baron," Vicky said in an attempt to change the subject to something a bit more comfortable. "He tried to blackmail me."

James turned to face her so suddenly, her breath caught. "Blackmail? What do you mean blackmail? How?"

Vicky sighed. "Apparently he learned what happened with Duncan. If I do not keep what I know about the affair he and the duchess are having, he has promised to reveal everything and thus drag the business and me through the mud."

"How dare he!" James said through clenched teeth. "And how did you respond?"

"I took your advice," she replied. "I gathered my strength and stood up to him. He was bluffing, of course. He revealed everything about where he was and all he did last night."

"If he ever threatens you again, I will have words with him. If he only knew what you have endured."

Vicky smiled and placed a hand on his arm. "It is over and there is no reason to cause a feud." This seemed to calm him, and she went on to explain all she had learned from Lord Gerard, ending with seeing Lady Warwick returning to her rooms much later than she said she had.

"Do you believe him?" James asked. "Do you really think he saw her?"

Vicky glanced over her shoulder at the marchioness, who stood speaking with her husband. "I do. Which leads me to wonder what she was doing walking around the house at such a late hour. I have my suspicions, but I must be more careful with my accusations." Her thoughts went to Richard, and she could not shake the feeling that there was more to the relationship between Richard and Lady Warwick.

Her head began to ache, and she rubbed a temple to ease the pain. All this investigating was hard work! She was glad she did not have to do it all the time.

James must have recognized her frustration, for he said, "Let me get you a glass of wine. This weekend was supposed to be one of leisure, not work."

"If I am to fulfill the duchess's request," Vicky said with a sigh, "I cannot enjoy another moment of leisure. I still have so much to investigate." She glanced toward the door. "It is a pity the constable is so incompetent. If he was able to do what is expected of him, I would not be in this position."

"I will not have you arguing with me," James said with light admonishment. "Either you accept a drink or I will embarrass us both. I am unsure how, but I promise to find a way. Perhaps I will sing some sort of sea shanty. That would make everyone turn to stare in our direction." He added a wink before walking over to the drinks table.

Vicky recognized how fortunate one could be to have a friend, but to have one as dear as James was a blessing. Her thoughts went back to the day she returned to her father's office, her heart broken. She had cried rivers of tears, and as her father was away that day, it was James who had comforted her.

When her father became ill, she spent many long hours working with James doubly hard so the clients would see they had no reason for concern. Not once did he ask for extra pay, although he put in far more hours than he ever had. And not once did he seek to take advantage of her as many men would have despite the fact he had every opportunity. And too often when the grief became too heavy, he would tell her to rest as he continued to work through the night while she slept.

"Vicky?"

She turned as James walked up to her. "Yes?"

"Are you all right?" he asked as he handed her a glass.

"Oh, yes," she replied, smiling. "I am well." She took a sip of the wine. "Remind me when we return to order a bottle of this."

James laughed. "I think when you learn the price of just a single bottle you may reconsider."

She joined in his laughter, but she wanted to speak to him about another issue. Where did they stand? She knew quite well what he felt for her, and for a moment she considered that perhaps they could become more than friends and colleagues.

"James," she said, looking into his kind face, "I wanted to discuss—"

"Is the music not the most wonderful you have ever heard?" Lady Warwick said as she walked up to them. "I find their talent to be the best in the area."

"They are quite good," Vicky replied. "And despite the tragedies of the past two days, this has been a perfect evening, my lady."

"I take pride in my ability to organize a wondrous gathering," the marchioness said. "Now, Mr. Kensington, I would like to speak to you alone if I may." It was a command and not a request.

"I will talk to you later," James whispered as the marchioness pulled him toward the door, leaving Vicky to stare after them.

"It appears you have lost him to another woman," Richard said with a laugh from behind her. "However, my arms are available if you wish to ease your pain."

Vicky turned to glare at him. "Only rogues and highwaymen speak to a woman's back," she said. "I have no doubt you are one of the two, yet it would not surprise me if you were both."

Richard placed a hand on his chest. "Your accusations hurt my soul, Miss Parker," he said dramatically. "And although you likely believe I am without a soul, I assure you I do have one."

"Oh, I do not doubt it," she replied. "But I suspect it is as black as the night sky."

He replied with a light chuckle and then looked past her. "That Gerard is always scheming," he said. "Even now I know he is devising some sort of dastardly plan. If only I knew what it was."

Vicky raised her brows. "Why? So you may join him?"

"Hardly," Richard replied with a snort. "What I want is to stay a step ahead of him. I do enjoy the game." He looked at her. "And I speak of more than business."

"Is that so?" Vicky replied with disdain. "I did not believe him your type." She could not help but revel in his hurt expression.

Now if James would hurry up and return to relieve her of her present company, she would be far happier.

Chapter Sixteen

Vicky was uncertain if the pounding in her head had worsened due to the wine she had thus far consumed, exhaustion from running her own inquest, or Richard's tendency to speak without ceasing.

When Lady Warwick and James returned, James relieved Vicky of the last problem by engaging Richard in conversation, and Lady Warwick conversed with the baron. Both were a welcomed relief.

Then Richard surprised her by turning toward her suddenly and saying, "I cannot remain polite any longer. You must allow me to call on you."

"I beg your pardon?" Vicky asked, taken aback.

"Do not think me a fool, but your eyes have not left me since our first encounter upon your arrival. Your propensity to mock and ridicule me is clearly an attempt at flirtation. You really should not be frustrated that you are attracted to me, for many women are. Therefore, allow me to call on you. Or better yet, why not allow me to show you the best sights of London."

Vicky wondered if Richard was as hard of hearing as Mr. Luntworth, an elderly gentleman of eighty who had been a client well before her father's passing. He carried a small tube that allowed him to hear what people were saying to him.

Or perhaps he was more like Lord Trickle, a scoundrel who undressed Vicky with his eyes each time he encountered her. Every time he visited the office, he would comment on her beauty and ask her to attend one function or another as his guest despite the fact she refused every time.

However, she suspected he was most like Lord Wasley. Just plain stubborn.

Well, two could play at that game! She gave him her best wide-eyed innocent look. "Would you take me to the theater?" she asked demurely.

Richard nodded. "Of course."

"And the museum, as well?"

Again he nodded, this time with more exuberance. "Most definitely. Whatever you wish, we shall do."

She gave him her sweetest smile. "And a picnic?"

"I cannot see why not. I will provide the finest selection of cheeses and the best wine."

Vicky pressed a hand to her breast and sighed. "You truly are a romantic," she said. "However, my greatest desire is to attend Astley's Circus."

To this, Richard furrowed his brow. "I must admit that I am surprised by such a request. Why would you wish to see the circus?"

"It is the home of wild beasts, is it not? And seeing you in your natural habitat would be quite entertaining." His dropped jaw left her with a feeling of great satisfaction. "Good evening to you, sir." And she walked away.

"Oh, James," she said with glee as she joined him, "I must tell you the most amusing story!"

He smiled at her. "Do tell!"

She went on to recount her conversation with Richard, dabbing tears of laughter from her eyes by the time she finished.

"That was brilliant!" James regaled. He glanced in Richard's direction. "It appears he is still in shock. Look!"

Indeed, Richard leaned against a far wall pouting, his arms crossed over his chest.

Serves him right, Vicky thought.

Her amusement was cut short, however, when a loud moan echoed through the room followed by the sound of shattering glass. The music stopped instantaneously, and all eyes turned to where the duchess lay in a heap.

Vicky and James hurried over, and Vicky prayed the woman had not been poisoned like her husband.

The baron lifted the duchess's head, placed it in his lap, and began fanning her. Her eyes fluttered as she came to.

"What is going on here?" Lady Warwick demanded, staring down at the pair, her hands planted on her hips. "Is she drunk?"

Lord Warwick knelt down beside them, concern etched on his features. "Charlotte? What happened?"

"I was thinking of my Felton and the dance we shared the day we were married," the duchess said in a weak voice. "And now my beloved is gone." Tears glistened in her eyes as Lord Gerard helped her stand. "I am sorry to ruin such a lovely evening."

"You have done no such thing," Lord Warwick replied. "Would you like to remain? Or would you prefer to retire for the night? I am sure our guests would not be insulted, not after all you have endured."

The duchess shook her head. "I believe I will go to the library and read. Perhaps after a short rest I will be able to rejoin the festivities." She brought her wrist to her forehead. "Although I am still a bit faint." As she held out her arms to balance herself, she tumbled toward the baron once more, who placed a protective arm around her waist.

"I shall escort her," the baron said. "I had hoped to select a book to read later, anyway, and this will give me the opportunity to do so."

"Yes, please do," Lord Warwick said. "And do not leave her alone in case she has another episode."

"Trust me," Lord Gerard said, "I will take good care of her."

Vicky had to hide a smile. The duchess – no both of them – should have gone into the theater.

Once the pair was gone and the music resumed, Lord Warwick let out a heavy sigh. Then he turned to Vicky and smiled. "Besides this small interlude," he said, "are you enjoying the evening thus far, Miss Parker?"

"Indeed, I am," Vicky replied. She glanced around them. "I have to say, this room is the most elegant in the house."

Lord Warwick smiled with clear pride. "I do like it. Lavinia has insisted it needs redecorating, but it is one room I have refused to see changed." When he smiled again, Vicky was reminded of a young boy rather than a grown man. "I will be sad to see you go, Victoria, but I do hope to invite you to a proper party in the near future."

"Do you?" Vicky asked in astonishment before covering her mouth. She dropped into a curtsy. "I mean, thank you, my lord." The shock did not leave her, however. An accountant's daughter simply did not receive invitations to parties given by the *ton*, and yet here she was receiving a second, even if it was only in passing.

Apparently, Vicky was not the only one surprised. "George," Lady Warwick hissed, "Miss Parker may be a friend, in the business sense, but I am sure she understands that our parties are strictly for those of the aristocracy." She gave Vicky an apologetic, although clearly forced, smile.

"Nonsense," Lord Warwick replied. "Dranford has attended Father's parties for forty years, and the man's holdings are whatever is in his hands at the time. No, you have told me to prepare myself for assuming Father's title, and I shall. Beginning with inviting whomever I choose to our social gatherings."

As the couple continued to argue, James took Vicky by the elbow and led her a short distance away. "It appears Lord Warwick grows tired of his wife dictating his life," James said with a tiny snicker. "I cannot say I blame him."

"Nor I," Vicky replied. "Now, what did you and Lady Warwick discuss? It was not her husband, was it?"

"We did," James said. "She wants me to convince him to leave for India. I told her I would do my best, but, Vicky, I do not feel comfortable in doing so." His tone became earnest.

"To be honest," Vicky said, "I do not believe it will matter. If tonight is any indication, Lord Warwick is ready to start making his own decisions."

To this, James laughed. "It should be interesting to see how she responds to that!"

Vicky grinned. "Very interesting, indeed."

***

The baron and duchess did not return to the party, and as the musicians began to store away their instruments, Vicky assumed the pair would remain hidden until morning.

Although her head ached more now than it had earlier, Vicky had yet to speak to Lady Warwick to learn the truth about where she had been the night before. Tact was key in moments like these, so after wishing James a good night for the evening, she squared her shoulders and approached the marchioness.

"What a relief I am able to serve drinks to my guests without worry they will die from consuming them," Lady Warwick said with a giggle when she saw Vicky. "I know I should not make light of what happened to my father-in-law, but I cannot seem to help myself!" She grabbed the edge of the table to steady herself. Clearly, she had consumed her fair share of drink.

The timing could not have been more perfect. Overconsumption of alcohol loosened the tongue quite well. "I was hoping we could speak alone," Vicky said with a warm smile.

"Oh, I would so enjoy that," Lady Warwick replied. She picked up a nearby glass of wine and downed it in one gulp, smacking her lips as she teetered on her feet. "Come. Let us go to the sitting room where we can be more comfortable."

Vicky took the marchioness by the arm to keep her upright as they made their way out of the ballroom.

"You know," Lady Warwick said as she patted Vicky's hand, "you are a good friend. I do hope you understand that my reason for not having you at our parties is not because of you specifically. It is just that those of your station would be most unwelcome by the majority of our guests. I would hate to see you hurt by their harsh treatment, which I am sure they would demonstrate." Vicky had to pay close attention to what the marchioness said, for the woman slurred her words terribly.

"I do understand," Vicky replied. "Appearances are important."

Lady Warwick patted Vicky's hand again. "I knew you would see my point. You really are quite perceptive."

As they passed the library, the marchioness glanced at the closed door. "I do hope they found a good book to read." She giggled. "Oh, what does it matter? Let the girl be happy."

When they arrived at the sitting room, Lady Warwick instructed Vicky to light several more candles from the few that were already lit.

Vicky did as requested, and soon the room was washed in light. The marchioness had poured herself another drink, sherry this time, and offered Vicky a glass.

"Thank you, but no," Vicky replied. "I am afraid I have consumed enough for one night."

Lady Warwick shrugged, took her glass over to the couch, and dropped unceremoniously onto it. "Come and sit with me," she said, patting the cushion beside her. "Tell me what hangs heavily on your heart."

Vicky took her seat, smoothing her skirts and wondering where to begin. Did she really wish to share her most intimate thoughts with this woman? And did the woman truly wish to hear them?

Deciding that neither was true, she said, "I enjoyed the party tonight. I understand you planned the entire thing. Does the duchess never take on her responsibilities?"

"The woman spends every available moment deciding when to act out her dramatics and how she will spend the duke's money." She grinned. "Which will be considerably less now that he is gone. But yes, I planned the entire weekend."

"Mr. Kent says that you would like your husband to take the journey his father was unable to take. Is that true?"

"Indeed," Lady Warwick replied. Then she scowled and leaned in closer, and Vicky had to stop herself from pulling away from the heavy odor of spirits on the woman's breath. "Richard is a rogue, you know. Be careful or you may fall for his charms."

"Thank you for the warning," Vicky said, annoyed at the change of direction the conversation was taking. "May I ask why you would like the marquess to leave? Will you not miss him?"

Lady Warwick drank from her glass and guided it to the table with exaggerated care. "You ask a very complicated question," she replied once she was upright once more. "One I ask myself often." She sighed and fell back against the cushions. "George is different from most men, and although that is not necessarily a bad thing, it does not make for a good duke. Despite his age and training, he is naive about most matters, making him a target for those looking to use him for their own gain. I cannot stand by any longer and watch. If he goes to India, say for a year, he will see new lands, live life, and meet new people, all experiences his father denied him. Perhaps he will become the man he needs to be. And while he is away, I shall rule over the estate and its holdings. If left to him in his current state, we will be destitute before the end of his first year as duke."

The pounding of Vicky's heart matched the pounding in her head. She was getting closer to the truth but it was imperative she learn more. "My lady, I see you care for your husband. You make every decision for him, all for his own good."

She held her breath as she waited for the marchioness's reaction. Making such statements could go one of two ways. Either the marchioness responded candidly, or Vicky was thrown out on her ear.

"What you say is true," Lady Warwick replied with a deep sigh, closing her eyes. "I must keep him safe. I will do anything for my George." The last was a low murmur. Would she fall asleep right there in the sitting room?

"I imagine you are the kind of woman who would stop at nothing. Am I right?"

The marchioness nodded without opening her eyes.

"I cannot help but wonder if the reason you wish to send him away is not so he will learn but rather to protect him."

Lady Warwick opened her eyes and stared. "Protect him from what?"

Vicky took the woman's hand in hers. "You were not in your room when the duke was murdered," she said. "You cannot deny this, for Lord Gerard saw you returning to your room quite late. You told me you had retired for the night immediately after catching Mr. Kent listening at the library door. Therefore, I have come to the conclusion that you witnessed your husband poisoning his father. Is it why you asked him to tell no one he purchased the bottle of brandy? You saw him poison it and do not wish to see him charged with murder."

By the time Vicky finished, the marchioness was sitting upright and sobbing. "No," she whispered. "My George would never..." Her words trailed off. Then she said, "What I saw, I cannot repeat, Miss Parker. You must understand, he is my husband. I must protect him as I always have! Now more than ever I am certain he must go to India. If you have figured out what he did, surely the constable will, as well." Her eyes went wide and she placed a hand over her mouth. "I did not mean...that is, if we assume George did what you believe he did, then others will make the same assumption."

"I cannot tell you what to do," Vicky said quietly, "but I would suggest that in the morning, allow me to speak to Lord Warwick. Perhaps I can use the guilt he must have as a way to get him to confess. Then the two of you will be able to put this all behind you." That was an outright lie. Murder was one of the few crimes that those of nobility could not use the privilege of peerage to keep them from prosecution, especially when it was a duke who was murdered.

"You would do that for me?" Lady Warwick asked.

Vicky nodded.

The marchioness wrung her hands. "And if he does not confess?"

"You must trust me. I believe Lord Warwick has a good heart and will tell the truth."

Lady Warwick dabbed at her eyes with a handkerchief. "If you think it best," she said, sniffling. "Then do as you must." She picked up her glass once more. "I would like to be alone with my thoughts if you do not mind."

"Of course," Vicky replied. She could not help but feel sorry for the woman. After all she had done for her husband, the thought of losing him had to weigh heavy on her.

Once in the corridor, Vicky pressed the heels of her hands to her temple. Her head was aching worse than it had all day. If she was to confront Lord Warwick, she would need a powder, and she knew right where to find one.

Chapter Seventeen

Vicky made her way to the kitchen where Mrs. Prowler was wiping off the last of the crumbs from the counter as she snapped orders to several of the younger kitchen maids. When she saw Vicky, she placed her hands on her hips and smiled.

"What can I do for you, miss? Would you like a pastry or something else to eat?"

"No, thank you," Vicky replied. "I am afraid my head is aching and I was hoping to find a powder Lady Warwick keeps in her medicine cabinet."

Mrs. Prowler chuckled. "Medicine cabinet, is that what she told you?" Vicky nodded. "Well, that might be what it's called, but she keeps more than headache powders in it." She motioned behind her with a thumb. "Back there on the left. The cabinet on the wall. She must trust you 'cause she don't even let her own husband get anything from it. He has to ask her to get it for him."

"Thank you," Vicky said, hoping the cook would not mention to the marchioness about this encounter. After all, Vicky had not asked permission beforehand. Yet, what harm would it be if she was able to get the relief she needed?

She made her way to a steel box with two doors on its front. She pulled on the bronze knobs. The cabinet was deeper than she had expected, allowing two rows of five bottles per shelf. However, they were not apothecary bottles, as she would have expected, but rather bottles of alcohol — wines, sherry, and even a few spirits she could not name.

Lord Warwick had alluded to his wife's overindulgence of liquor, but Vicky had no idea how terrible the woman's problem was. If she hid away this much liquor, she had a terrible problem, indeed!

On the bottom shelf, Vicky found a selection of apothecary bottles, a small coin purse, and the pouches of powders she sought. Taking one, she looked over the contents of the cabinet once more and then closed the doors.

When she returned to Mrs. Prowler, the older woman threw her cleaning cloth on the counter and said, "There. Another late night, but my kitchen's clean." She glowered at the back of one of the scullery maids reaching inside one of the great pots. "And that despite the lazy chits they give me to help." She shook her head and wiped her hands on her apron. "Now, did you find what you needed?"

"I did, thank you," Vicky replied. "Not to gossip, but does the marchioness come into the kitchen often for medicine?"

Mrs. Prowler grinned. "I do love me a bit of gossip," she whispered, glancing at the scullery maid once more. "She does come to get her drinks, but we're supposed to act like we don't notice. Why, only last night she came to get something, and when I asked if I could speak to her about the next market order, I thought she'd tear my head off. I've never seen her act like that before. She was so angry, she forgot to take a bottle with her!"

"Well, the fact you still have your position says that she was not angry enough to throw you out," Vicky said.

"Might be a blessing if she did," Mrs. Prowler said with a laugh.

"Then you'd just complain about not havin' work."

"What was that, Jenny?" Mrs. Prowler asked.

The scullery maid crawled out of the pot, her face a bright red. "Nothin', Mrs. Prowler. I was just complainin' about how much work I have."

Mrs. Prowler snorted. "Insolent chit," she said but with more affection than anger. "She does do good work, though, so I guess I can put up with her sass." She turned back to Vicky. "Are you sure you don't want something to eat? I can make whatever you'd like."

"I appreciate the offer, but I will take this powder and retire for the night."

Wishing the cook a good evening, Vicky left the kitchen. In the foyer, she heard footsteps and saw Lady Warwick stumbling toward her room. She clearly had consumed a great deal more alcohol after Vicky had left the sitting room, for she was close to crawling up the stairs. Vicky hoped the woman would not be too ill the following morning.

Once the marchioness was out of sight, Vicky went to the library, hoping no one was there. She gave a quiet knock, counted to five, and entered. To her relief, it was empty.

"What are you doing?"

Vicky jumped and turned around. "Oh, James, you startled me!"

"My apologies," James said as he walked up to her. "I was speaking to Mr. Kent when I saw you come in here."

A hand still pressed against her breast, Vicky laughed. "No, you are fine." She picked up one of the candles and went to a bookshelf.

"I thought your head was aching," James said.

"It is," she replied. "However, I plan to confront Lord Warwick tomorrow before we leave, and before I can do that, I must verify something first."

"Then you do believe he did it!" James said. "What did you learn?"

Vicky glanced at the door and took a step closer to him. "It all came together after I spoke with the marchioness tonight." She explained the conversation she and Lady Warwick had shared. "I cannot do this last part on my own. Will you help me?"

"There is no need to ask," James replied. "I would never refuse you any request."

For a brief moment, Vicky imagined opening up her heart to this man and taking the path toward love once more. How wonderful it would be to experience such feelings again.

"Then let us begin," she said, smiling. "Together."

She explained what she was searching for, and they perused the shelves until James said, "Here. You can start with this."

Taking the book he offered her, she went to the couch while he continued looking. After several minutes, she closed the book and chose another from the growing pile beside her.

Hours seemed to pass until Vicky finally closed a particular book in her hands. "It is as I thought," she said. "Tomorrow, this will all come to an end."

"So you found what you were searching for?"

"Indeed."

"I knew you would," he said. "I never doubted it for a moment."

Vicky went to stand, but the room spun around her.

James hurried to her side. "You must get some rest," he said. "Why not retire for the night? There is nothing you can do right now."

She glanced at the books piled around them. "But this mess," she said. "I must—"

"I will take care of this," he said. "You need to rest."

Vicky smiled. "Thank you."

When she reached the door, she turned to watch as James gathered several books in his arms and went to one of the shelves. She admired his unwavering dedication to her and prayed that one day she would be able to return the same.

Chapter Eighteen

The sun was just above the horizon as Vicky peered out the window of her assigned bedroom. The storm from the night before had passed, as had the aching in her head. Feeling rejuvenated, she had already dressed, ready to confront Lord Warwick.

Making her way downstairs, she caught sight of the baron entering the library. It was her guess that the duchess was likely inside waiting for him. Why the pair believed no one suspected them of having an affair was beyond her, but what they did was not her concern. Revealing the person who had murdered the duke was.

She walked to the study and found Lord Warwick standing at the window staring outside. He turned and smiled when she entered.

"Ah, Victoria, please, come in. The weekend passed all too quickly. I admit that I will be sad to see you go."

Vicky dropped into a curtsy. "Thank you," she replied. "And I will be sad to leave." She paused. "I wished to speak to you concerning an important matter. Do you have a moment?"

The marquess nodded, walked past her, and closed the door. "Please, have a seat. Is there a problem? You are well, are you not?"

"Yes, I am well, thank you," she replied, although everything would not be well once she said her piece. "As you know, I have been doing my own inquest into the murder of your father. I hope you do not think me impertinent, but I have a few more questions I would like to ask you."

"Constable Cogwell assured me not ten minutes ago that he is quite close to solving Father's murder," Lord Warwick said. Then he shook his head. "But I do not believe he truly is. He seems a bit... How can I put this delicately? And please do not judge me, but the only word that comes to mind is inept."

Vicky smiled. "I would agree, but I ask that you do not judge me, either. My lord—"

"George, please."

"George," Vicky parroted, still finding it difficult to address a soon-to-be duke so informally. "I understand that you are considering going to India. Have you decided whether or not you will go?"

The marquess chuckled. "Lavinia believes it will be good for me, and Richard has also said as much. In truth, I have not decided. I would miss my wife dearly if I were to go, but if I return a better man, perhaps it would be well worth the time away."

"A better man how?" Vicky asked, leaning forward. "I see you as a capable gentleman, a man worthy of the dukedom."

Lord Warwick smiled. "You are very gracious, but I lack insight in matters of business. Simple tasks a man must complete daily seem to fail me. Or so says my wife. As did my father." His face fell. "There are times when I would like to prove to her that I am capable of much more than she believes, that she does not need to control my life. Father kept a firm rein on everything I have done since I was old enough to think, but now I realize why he insisted I marry her."

"So she could continue his work." Vicky understood all too well, for she felt very much the same way. If only people would see that she was just as capable as James, even if she was a woman.

"Exactly!" the marquess said, his voice rising. "Were you aware that Lavinia even shops for all my clothing? Of course, I go into the tailor's pretending I know what I want, but it is all a ruse." He sighed. "My entire life is a ruse."

"But was it not you who selected the brandy for your father?"

Lord Warwick laughed outright. "I find it easy to speak with you, Victoria," he said. "You are open and forthright with your words, and that is a comfort. As to your question, no. It was Lavinia who ordered it, and she kept it in her medicine cabinet in the kitchen." He snorted. "And do not believe I was allowed anywhere near that! It is restricted, even for me. And then there is Mrs. Prowler."

An image of the sturdy cook came to Vicky's mind. "What about Mrs. Prowler?"

"The woman controls that kitchen better than Saint Peter controls the gates to Heaven!" he said with a grin. "No one enters unless she allows them. Even me, the duke's son, cannot go in there without receiving a severe tongue lashing."

Vicky clasped her hands tightly, hoping the marquess would not notice her nervousness. "The night of your father's death, you met with him at eleven o'clock. It was then that you gifted him the bottle of brandy."

Lord Warwick sighed heavily. "Yes, I had hoped that the brandy could be a peace offering. I wanted him to see that I am as capable as he was." A deep scowl crossed his face. "Why could he not see me as the man I truly am? No one does, and it upsets me more than you can imagine." His face darkened further. "I gave him the brandy, which he accepted without hesitation. Then he began to pour two drinks. 'Let us celebrate as men do,' he insisted, although he knows very well that I do not consume alcohol. When I refused, he became so irate that he ordered me out of his presence. He has never done that before! Oh, he ridiculed me for my decision to abstain, but he never threw me out because of it."

Vicky considered all Lord Warwick had told her. Was it possible the duke meant to murder his son? Yet why would he wish to see his heir dead? No duke in his right mind would end the lineage simply to spite a son he felt was unworthy. Not with a wife who could guide his hand. That only left this man as the most likely culprit.

Then why did the duke respond to Lord Warwick's refusal with such venom if he knew all too well that his son did not drink?

"And so you returned to your bed," Vicky continued for him, "angry at your father and plotting ways to make him see you for who you truly are. You even used a business deal to prove your worth to Lord Gerard, as well."

"I...well, yes," Lord Warwick said, surprised. "Gerard believes he outwitted me, that I accepted his proposition simply because he wanted me to. However, I am much more capable of making decisions than that."

"I may be a woman and know little about the requirements of a duke," Vicky said, "but I can see you will make a fine duke. I imagine that it was your intention that once the deal is set, even your wife will be forced to recognize your competency. Am I correct in saying so?"

"It is as if you know me!" Lord Warwick said with a grin that went from ear to ear. "Perhaps better than I know myself!"

"I understand what it is like to be thought of as less than you are," Vicky replied. "But that is neither here nor there. I heard that you requested the baron take the brandy to the library and hide it. Why the baron? Was it a way to demonstrate the authority you have over him?"

"I had to find a way to get the bottle from my bedroom to a place from where I could retrieve it later without being caught doing so. Giving gifts can be so complicated sometimes." He shook his head at this. "But I suppose I can admit that there was the thrill in seeing Gerard willing to do my bidding." His eyes widened. "It was the baron who had the bottle last, or at least before I took it from the library to my father. You do not think--."

"I do not want to accuse him just yet," Vicky replied. She said nothing about Richard being the one who had moved the bottle to the library. "But I do have one last question I would like to ask. If the murderer is found, are you concerned about the rumors that may arise in the days ahead because of them?"

Lord Warwick snorted. "What do I care about rumors? Gossip abounds no matter how much one tries to stop it. Even if there was nothing about which to gossip, one person or another would simply make up something out of sheer boredom."

"You may as well know that once the world learns the truth, I am afraid there will be no stopping the rumor wheel."

He stood. "Are you saying that you know who killed my father?"

"I am."

"Then I will send word to everyone to meet in the sitting room in one hour. Is that enough time?"

Vicky smiled. "That is just the right amount of time," she said.

"You seem very confident. Are you certain you know who the killer is?"

"I am positive," Vicky replied. She turned to leave but then stopped. "One last thing. Can you see that tea is sent up, as well? We must have tea."

***

Twenty minutes remained until the meeting would begin as Vicky paced the floor of her room. Her heart pounded in her chest and air refused to enter her lungs. Would she faint before she had the chance to make her pronouncement? What she needed was a breath of fresh air, and so she hurried downstairs and out to the gardens.

The sun shone brightly, warming her as she drew in great amounts of breath in order to calm herself, but her face still felt flushed. Why did speaking in front of people bring her so much distress?

She knew why, at least in this case. What if she was wrong? Her accusation would not only bring about rebuke, but it might even ruin what she had been able to retain after her father's death. To accuse someone of murder was bad enough, but to wrongly accuse a member of the *ton*? Why, that was outrageous.

If she was wrong.

But what if she was correct in her guess? The duke's death would be avenged once the true murderer was brought to light. Plus, was what she believed merely a guess or was it based on specific evidence that pointed to the culprit? She was certain it was the latter.

What would be the best way to reveal the culprit? Should she point an accusatory finger at the start or slowly reveal what she knew?

Would it be best to include why everyone was a suspect and then divulge the most likely person to have committed the murder? Or did she reveal the name of the murderer followed by her findings to support her accusation?

These thoughts and more spun about in her mind, making her dizzy, which did not help her nervousness in any way.

A familiar figure joined her. "It is nearly time," James said. "Lord Warwick is speaking with the butler, but the rest of the party is already in the sitting room. Is it your plan to keep them waiting in order to make the murderer nervous before revealing your findings?"

If he only knew how much more nervous she was compared to whoever committed murder! "Oh, James, I cannot do this!" she blurted as she grasped the sleeve of his coat as if it would keep her from drowning. "I have revealed to you everything there is to know. Why not do it for me? Will you reveal the murderer? I would not mind if you took all the credit for it, either. Just do not make me speak in front of all those people!" She placed a hand to her stomach and glanced around for the best place to empty its contents, although she had nothing in it to retch.

"Since I have known you," James said in a calm tone as he smiled down at her, "I have never refused anything you have asked of me."

Relief washed over her. She would not be forced to endure everyone's eyes staring at her. "And I can never thank you enough for everything you do. Now, we should discuss what you will say—"

"But," he interrupted, "I cannot this time. It is you who has done all the work, who questioned every person, who put together the pieces of the puzzle. Therefore, it is you who should share what you have learned."

"You know how nervous I am when speaking in public," she said. "If there is any time I need your aid, it is today, now."

He brought her hand to his lips. "I spoke to you earlier about your fears. Do you remember?"

Vicky swallowed hard but nodded just the same. "I do."

"Once you embark on this path, it becomes nearly impossible to leave it. You are more than capable of what must be done." He lifted an arm. "Look at my hand. For years I have tried to hide it, for it makes me believe I am a lesser man because of the fingers it lacks."

"But you are not," Vicky insisted. "You are more a gentleman, more a man, than most men anywhere could hope to be. Even those with titles."

He chuckled. "That may be true, but my fear of ridicule sent me down the path of a coward. Lately, however, I see a new path, one upon which I have decided I belong. And it is because of you that I make that choice, for I see your strength and covet it. Now, you may go inside and address the party, but if you still believe you cannot, I will do it for you. However, you must ask yourself one thing: is this truly the path you wish to take?"

Old wounds that had lain dormant tore open once more. Did this man not realize what his words did to her? Yet, they also forced her to consider the truth. What did she truly fear? Speaking before a group of people who knew little about her? Or was her fear rooted in something else, something closer to her heart?

And as if a candle had been lit in a dark room, she realized that her dread stemmed from a place beyond simple fear. Oh, yes, she still worried that she would muddle her words, but it was as she had told Lord Warwick. She was certain who murdered the duke, so there was no reason for concern that she would point at the wrong person.

Vicky wiped tears from her eyes. "I am tired of living in fear," she said, straightening her back. "I will speak for myself."

"And I will be there with you," James said. "If at any time you feel as if you cannot speak, just look at me. I trust you to tell the truth, and the truth always prevails."

"Thank you," she said, embracing him.

Although she did not want it to end, the embrace broke, and James glanced toward the house. "'It will be a weekend of leisure,' she said. 'A well-deserved break.'" He shook his head. "That is the last time I listen to you, Miss Victoria Parker!"

Vicky gasped in mock affront as he walked away. "Mr. Kensington, you apologize to me at once or I will see you booted to the curb with no wages!"

James laughed as he offered her his arm, and together, they entered the house, Vicky's steps firmer than they had been when she had slipped outside for air.

Chapter Nineteen

As Vicky entered the drawing room, all conversation ended and everyone turned to Vicky. She had to force every muscle to move, to propel her forward and not carry her away screaming in terror. Yet, when her eyes fell on James, his smile reminded her that she had nothing to fear.

"I do hope this will not take long," Lord Gerard grumbled. "The morning is far too pleasant to spend indoors, and I was hoping to get in a spot of fishing before I return home."

"You are welcome to go," Vicky said, surprised that her voice revealed none of her inner turmoil. "However, what I have to say concerns you as much as everyone present."

The baron frowned but walked over to sit in an empty chair. Lady Warwick sat beside the duchess on the couch, and Richard had taken one of the wing-back chairs beside the empty fireplace. When she glanced in his direction, he smiled at her. She ignored him.

Vicky closed her eyes and conjured the words she had practiced over and again as she and James returned to the house. Yes, she was ready.

"Thank you all for coming," she said. "Since the death of the duke—"

"Forgive me for my tardiness!" Constable Cogwell interrupted as he hurried into the room. His hair was disheveled and he was buttoning his coat. Had the man run down the corridor? "I was…investigating in the kitchen."

A snort echoed Vicky's thoughts. Is that what he called eating these days? Yet, she could not blame the man. How often did he have the opportunity to partake in the wonderful cuisine provided by a grand house such as Stanting Estate? Likely never.

Vicky made no comment to the constable but instead continued with her prepared speech. "As I was saying, since the duke's death, I too have been making inquiries into his murder. More specifically, I have been looking into who had access to the bottle of brandy that contained the poison that killed him, who would wish him dead, and who had the opportunity to do so."

The baron laughed as he stood once more. "I have no desire to listen to the ramblings of a woman with little or no breeding." He turned to Lord Warwick. "Will you allow your guests to suffer listening to this prattle?"

"Oh, do sit down, Gerard!" Lord Warwick snapped to everyone's amazement. "Victoria is as much a guest in my home as you and has done more to learn who killed my father than anyone." He glanced at the constable. "My apologies, Cogwell."

The constable's eyes were wide. "None taken, my lord."

"And as she said to you before," continued the marquess, "you are welcome to leave. However, I will warn you now. If you do choose to leave before she has revealed her findings, you will not be invited back."

The baron, his entire face so red he appeared on the verge of having a stroke, retook his seat.

"Now, George," Lady Warwick admonished, "there is no reason to raise your voice. It is unbecoming of the man who will soon take his place as the Duke of Everton."

Vicky drew in a deep breath, wishing her nerves would settle. How was she ever to finish what she had to say if she kept getting interrupted?

She bent her head to Lord Warwick to acknowledge his trust in her. "Thank you, my lord. Now, as I was saying. Everyone here has a motive for murdering His Grace, yet just because one has a motive does not mean one committed murder."

She looked at Lord and Lady Warwick. "Some will receive a great inheritance. Some will have new opportunities for business."

Richard shifted in his seat, and Lord Gerard found a sudden interest in folding his handkerchief.

She looked at the duchess. "And some will earn freedom. Each motive is as strong as the next. Have no doubt, every one of you lied initially about his or her whereabouts the night of the duke's murder, for each of you has something to hide."

The duchess's eyes widened. "Miss Parker, surely there is no need…" Her words trailed off and she looked down at her hands once more.

"Unlike most, I have no interest in the private goings-on here or in any other household. And since much of what was revealed to me was done so in confidence and has little or nothing to do with why the duke was murdered, I shall keep the particulars of those details to myself."

A collective sigh filled the room.

"Now, on to the motives that do pertain to the duke's murder." This made more than one person tense again. She turned to the duchess. "Although Her Grace cared for her husband, it is not a secret that she did not love him. However, this is not all that uncommon. Marriage, at least with those in the nobility, has been seen as nothing more than a contractual agreement for generations, putting together more than one couple who never learned to love one another."

Constable Cogwell gave a sad nod.

"Lady Warwick has been given a great deal of responsibility," Vicky said, turning her gaze on the marchioness. "So much so that any woman in her place might be driven to murder." She looked at the baron. "Or perhaps it was the collapse of a business arrangement that forced someone's hand."

"It is just as I suspected," the constable said. "It is always the baron." Vicky clicked her tongue and the man fell silent once more.

"Then there is the man whose reputation proceeds him." She said this as she turned her gaze on Richard Kent.

"They are nothing more than rumors," Richard insisted. "I assure you, I am nothing like the man people believe me to be."

"I speak only of your love of reading scripture," Vicky replied with a sly grin. "Is that not your reputation?"

Several people snickered, and Richard's cheeks reddened.

"Then we have the marquess, a man who wanted nothing more than to please his father."

The door opened and the butler entered with a heavily ladened tray. Light glinted off the highly polished silver tea set, and Vicky felt a surge of anticipation as he set the tray on the table.

"That will be all, Sheplin," she said. "I shall pour. Thank you."

The butler looked both shocked and offended, but he bowed and left the room in as much a huff as a butler could manage without being outright rude.

"I believe I speak for everyone when I say that this tea is the finest I have ever had," Vicky said as she poured the first cup of tea and handed it to Lady Warwick. "I assume you chose this particular blend, my lady."

"I did," the marchioness said as her nose raised slightly. "Only a handful of households in England have the means to secure such a rare blend."

Vicky then poured for the duchess. "I imagine that given the opportunity, you would have ordered this very blend yourself, would you not, Your Grace?"

The duchess smiled. "I imagine I would have," she replied, shooting a quick glare at the marchioness.

Vicky smiled and handed the next cup to Richard. She could not lie and say she had not considered spilling the entire cup in his lap just out of spite.

Once she had poured tea for the remaining attendees, Vicky took one for herself. "Now, before I reveal who the murderer is, I have something I believe will make this already marvelous tea all the more flavorful. My lady, would you do the honors of testing my theory?"

"Of course," Lady Warwick said with a wide smile. "I enjoy trying new flavors."

Vicky walked over to the marchioness, pulled out a tiny vial she had procured the night before, and poured half its contents into the teacup the marchioness held up to her. "There," she said. "Tell me if the flavor meets your high standards."

All the blood drained from Lady Warwick's face. "I-I am afraid I do not feel well," she stammered. Tea sloshed over the sides of the teacup as she lowered it to the table. "My stomach has been quite upset all morning."

Lord Warwick sat upright. "My love?" he said. "Are you certain? Perhaps a small sip will help rather than upset it further."

"I told you no, you fool!" the marchioness snapped. "Will you not listen to me?"

Vicky glanced at James, who gave her a nod of encouragement. "Or perhaps," she said, turning her attention once more to Lady Warwick, "you do not wish to drink it because you know it is poison?"

Lady Warwick sputtered, "That is preposterous! How dare you accuse me so! You, nothing more than a low-class spinster! George, I want this woman thrown out of my house this very instant!"

Vicky's heart thudded in her chest as the marquess looked at her. This was the moment of truth. Would the marquess do as his wife bade and throw Vicky out by her ear?

Constable Cogwell stepped forward. "Shall I see Miss Parker out, my lord?"

Lord Warwick rubbed his chin, still staring at Vicky as if she were some portrait on display. "No, that will not be necessary," he said finally. "She is to remain. Please, Miss Parker, continue."

In a fit of rage, his wife leaped from her seat. "I will not be insulted in front of our guests any longer! If you will not throw her out, then I shall retire to my room until she is gone."

Lord Warwick rose and glared down at the marchioness. "You will sit down and remain quiet, Lavinia!" he commanded. "And if you do not, I shall replace you with a wife who will!"

Lady Warwick's gasp resounded throughout the entire room, and she dropped into her seat like a sack of potatoes. "Well, I never…"

She glanced at her husband, who continued to glare at her, and pursed her lips shut.

Richard stared in amazement. The baron chuckled, and the duchess clasped her hands in delight.

Vicky, feeling more confident than she had since her arrival at Stanting Estate, raised the vial so everyone could see its label. "This came from Lady Warwick's private medicine cabinet in the kitchen. I found it last night when I went in search of a powder for an ache in my head. I had never heard of prussic acid and had to spend several hours in the library researching it. What I learned was that, in smaller doses, it is used as a sedative, but in higher dosages, the results can be deadly. If enough is used, the reaction is instantaneous."

The marchioness blanched further but seemed unable to respond.

"Now, according to Mrs. Prowler, the cook, no one is allowed to retrieve anything from the cabinet, including her own husband, without Lady Warwick's direct authorization. Is that true, my lord?"

Lord Warwick, who was scowling down at the floor mumbled, "That is correct."

"At first, I had thought the poison that killed His Grace had been put in the brandy at an earlier point in the day, or even earlier in the week. And learning how many people had handled the bottle left me greatly concerned. How was I to determine who had poisoned it and when? Yet, once I learned the duke's schedule for the night, as well as the whereabouts of everyone when he was murdered, it became evident who it was."

"It could have been you just as well as anyone," Lady Warwick retorted.

"That is true," Vicky replied. "I did have the opportunity, just as much as anyone else. However, I am one of two people, Mr. Kensington being the second, who had nothing to gain by the duke's death. You, Lady Warwick, did, however. During dinner the night of the duke's murder, you excused yourself to go for a headache powder."

"And what does that prove?" the marchioness demanded.

"Nothing on its face," Vicky said. "However, it did give you the chance to retrieve this bottle." She held up the vial of poison. "You then went to the library where Mr. Kent had stored the bottle and poisoned it. During your meeting, you informed the duke that Lord Warwick wished to share a drink with him, something His Grace had desired for a very long time. But you also knew full well that your husband would never accept an offer to drink and would be safe from ingesting the poison."

"This is utter nonsense!" Lady Warwick snapped as she stood once more.

"Sit down!" the marquess hissed.

Lady Warwick's eyes went wide, and she lowered herself into her seat once more.

"Go on, Victoria."

"Thank you," Vicky replied. "Now, you told me that you returned to your room soon after your meeting to find your husband snoring. However, Lord Warwick's appointment was immediately after yours, so that was a lie. Then, Lord Gerard saw you returning to your room an hour after your appointment with the duke ended, just as the alarm was raised, which begs the question, why were you up and about so late at night?"

"This is my home!" the marchioness said. "I have no curfew. If I choose to go for a glass of warm milk, no one has any reason to stop me."

"But you did not go for a glass of warm milk, did you?" Vicky demanded. "You waited in the shadows of the main floor to ascertain that your handiwork produced the results you hoped. You see, you could not pour in too little poison or he would simply be sedated and wake after a full night's sleep. Too much and he would be dead before he was to meet with those with later appointments. If he did not drink at all, however, there was no chance of him dying. Therefore, you listened at the library door to make certain the occupants would not be leaving anytime soon and then went to the study to see whether or not the duke had indeed drunk the brandy.

Once you were sure he had, you then went to the kitchen to return the remaining poison to the medicine cabinet before finally retiring for the night."

Lord Warwick rose from his seat once more and glared down at his wife. "That was why Father was so shocked when I refused his drink. You told him it was what I wanted!"

"She is lying!" Lady Warwick cried. "I did no such thing. Please, my love, you must believe me!"

"I added a healthy measure from this vial to her tea, enough needed to kill someone instantaneously. That is why she refused to drink."

"But what do I have to gain from the death of my father-in-law?" Lady Warwick demanded. "We receive more than enough allowance, and my husband would have received the dukedom eventually. Why would I want him to die sooner rather than later?"

It was the duchess's turn to leap from her chair. "She did not wish to wait to become the new duchess! She has been jealous of me since Felton and I married and it drove her to murder!"

"Is it because Father did not trust me enough?" Lord Warwick asked, dazed. "Is that why?"

Vicky shook her head. "Not necessarily," she replied. "But it was about control, what was to be gained. What Her Grace says closest to the truth. Lady Warwick was tired of waiting for what she saw as her just rewards. After all, she had been playing the part of Duchess of Everton without yet possessing the actual title."

"Enough!" Lady Warwick roared. "Yes, I poisoned the old fool! He wished to leave for India and take with him his title and wealth. The man would have lived another thirty years, content to do so in that godforsaken country! And where would that have left me? I have waited for so long to become the Duchess of Everton and for my husband to become the duke." She turned to Lord Warwick. "Do you not see, my love? With my help, you will become the greatest duke that ever lived, for I know what needs to be done. You need someone to run your life as I have run both this estate and the one we have in London.

No one can plan a party or host a weekend better than I!" She shot the duchess a glare. "Especially a snippet of a girl such as she."

"I have heard enough," the marquess said with a sigh. "Constable?"

Lady Warwick let out a sob and threw her arms around her husband, but he pried them away.

Constable Cogwell stared, a stupefied look on his face. "My lord?"

"Please escort my wife to the study until the proper authorities arrive to collect her. I want her out of my sight. And if I never see her again, it will be too soon."

"George?" Lady Warwick cried as the constable led her toward the door. "I did this all for you! Do you not see? It was the only way to see you got what you deserved!"

"And yet you wished to send me away?" the marquess replied. "I will never again believe a word that falls from your lips."

The room fell eerily quiet, the only sounds the distant shrieks of the marchioness as she was led down the corridor.

Vicky glanced around the room. The duchess beamed and Lord Gerard appeared stunned. James, however, winked at her.

Lord Warwick lowered himself into his seat. When he looked up at Vicky, his face was sad, and rightfully so. "Miss Parker, thank you for what you have done. I am in your debt."

"If it means anything," Vicky replied, "I am sorry." She did feel pity for the kind man, but she also felt a sense of pride for all she had been able to determine. And it was a wonderful feeling indeed.

Chapter Twenty

A gentle summer breeze caused the tiny hairs that peeked out from beneath Vicky's bonnet to tickle her face. Her hand lay on the arm of Lord Warwick as he walked her to the carriage where James stood patiently waiting at the door.

"I imagine this was not the weekend of leisure you thought it would be," Lord Warwick said as he glanced at her. "But I am glad you were here and thankful for what you have done. My father's soul will now rest peacefully because of what you were able to do here. My soul may need a little time to work itself through what has transpired, but hopefully with time I will find solace."

"Although it saddens me that the situation was placed before me, I am pleased to have been of aid," Vicky replied. A figure hurried toward them, and she lowered her voice. "I suppose Constable Cogwell does not share in your gratification, however."

The marquess chuckled as the constable came to stand before them. "Cogwell," Lord Warwick said. "I was just telling Miss Parker how much I have appreciated her input into all that has happened. Do you not agree that she is worthy of such praise?"

Constable Cogwell blanched and his eyes widened as he sputtered, "I hope you are not insinuating that I plan to exclude her actions from my report, my lord!"

"Now, why would I do that?" Lord Warwick asked. "Everyone here knows what she contributed to your inquest."

Constable Cogwell flinched. "Indeed, my lord," he replied. "I have every intention of including exactly what occurred, including all Miss Parker did to aid in the inquest. The truth is that I had come to the same conclusion as she, but she came forward first. I, on the other hand, prefer to have everything in perfect order before revealing what I know. That way I do not make false accusations." He said the last with a pointed look at Vicky.

Lord Warwick placed a hand on the constable's shoulder and said, "I would be careful that you include only relevant information, Cogwell."

The constable had gone so white he could have blended into the pebbles on the driveway, but he nodded all the same. "Y-yes, my lord. Only what is relevant."

Vicky knew the constable was in need of assurance, and rightly so. He must have felt a right fool to have a woman, one who was known as nothing more than an assistant to an accountant, usurp him in such a terrible way. "I was merely your assistant in your inquest, constable. You are the one who will present the findings to the barristers."

Lord Warwick seemed to appreciate her approach, for he winked at her.

The constable beamed with pleasure at her words, and Vicky had to turn away before she was overcome with laughter.

"Well, I must collect my things," Constable Cogwell proclaimed. "If you require my services again, my lord, please do not hesitate to call on me." He gave an awkward bow and then walked away, leaving Vicky and Lord Warwick alone once more.

"Truly, Victoria, I am in your debt for what you did here. Therefore, I must reward you. Name anything you wish, and I will grant it. Would you like some form of payment? A line of credit at one of the many dress shops in London? Or perhaps one of my finest thoroughbreds? I know! A country cottage for you in which to spend your holidays. Whatever you desire, it is yours."

His offer was tempting, for Vicky had little. Yet, there were more important things in life than material possessions, and one of them was friendship.

"My closest friends call me Vicky, my lord," she said, smiling. "Therefore, my wish is that you also call me Vicky. The honor of considering you as one of my closest friends is more than enough reward."

"Your wish is granted," the marquess said. "And please know that it is I who is honored. However, I must insist that I will only agree to address you as Vicky if you will do as I have already asked – twice, mind you! – and address me as George."

She laughed. "Then it is settled, George." His name did not stick to her tongue this time.

"Now, Vicky, know that this is not the last time we shall see one another. I must warn you that I invite my friends to visit often, either here at Stanting Estate or at my London home. I hope you will accept any or all of my future invitations."

Vicky dropped a curtsy. This was a great honor, indeed "I have no doubt I will," she replied. "Thank you."

As Vicky turned toward the carriage, the marquess added, "If there comes a time when you need my aid, I am here, no matter what the issue may be."

"I will keep that in mind," Vicky replied. "If the day comes, I will call upon you."

He glanced to his right. "It appears Kent wishes to speak with you," he whispered. "Would I be wrong in assuming he has romantic notions toward you?"

Vicky followed the marquess's gaze to see Richard leaning against a tree, his arms crossed over his chest. It appeared he was indeed watching her, and a new thought came to mind.

"You would not be wrong in your assumption," she said. "You know, George, if I may be so bold, may I make one more request of you?"

"Of course," he replied easily. "As I said, you are welcome to make any request you wish."

***

It was late afternoon when Vicky and James arrived at the accounting office on Wellington Street. James was still laughing as he closed the door behind them.

"I have never seen a man so pale!" he said, hanging the key on the hook beside the door. "But who can blame him? If I had been told that pestering you was akin to insulting the Crown and committing treason, I would have looked very much the same!"

Vicky joined in his laughter as she set her bag on the floor and began to remove her cloak. "It was kind of George to speak to him on my behalf," she said, placing the cloak on a nearby peg. "What a relief it is to know that Richard will keep away from me. I must be honest, after this weekend, I worried he would come skulking at my door whenever the feeling took him."

She had informed George that Richard had been nagging her, wishing her to grant him permission to call on her. The soon-to-be duke assured her that he would right that situation. And although she had no desire to wish him harm, the way he wiped the sweat from his brow and sent her fervent glances when the marquess spoke to him assured her that the scoundrel would not bother her again.

James walked over to the desk and began rummaging through a pile of papers. "I may do a bit of work before I go home," he said without looking up at her. "An hour of work now saves me an hour of work tomorrow."

Vicky clicked her tongue at him. "Go home and get some rest," she insisted. "There will always be work that needs completing. Besides, you had little time for leisure this weekend, and I certainly will be paying you for putting in an extra hour tonight!"

He chuckled. "Very well, if you wish to be rid of me, I will go." He walked to the door and stopped. "You know, I may go for a drink. Yes, a bit of ale does sound good after a weekend of all those fancy drinks."

Vicky frowned. "I thought you did not like public houses."

"That was nothing more than an excuse to not be around people, like many I used to make. However, there is no need to make excuses any longer. It is time I changed my path. After all, I am the only one capable of doing so."

He pulled the door open, and Vicky called out to him. "James?"

When he turned back to face her, her heart pounded. Not from fear but from something more, something different.

"After your help and encouragement this weekend," she said, choosing her words carefully, "I feel that thank you is not enough."

He shrugged. "It is as the marquess said. Being able to call you Vicky is honor enough. There is no need for thank yous." He gave her a bow. "Good evening to you, Miss Parker."

She dropped into a curtsy, giggling. "And to you, Mr. Kensington."

When the door closed, Vicky went to the window to watch James walk down the footpath. She remained there until he disappeared from sight. With a sigh, she turned and looked over the office. How different it felt when James was not present. It left her with a feeling she did not like.

Epilogue

Nearly a fortnight had passed since Vicky and James returned from their strange weekend at Stanting Estate, and the rumors concerning the death of the Duke of Everton had yet to abate. Some of the gossip circulating told the truth, that it was Lady Warwick who had murdered her father-in-law. Others, however, blamed his death on a cousin no one knew existed, a man who wished to exact revenge on the duke for a variety of reasons. Vicky found the latter much more amusing since no long-lost cousins had attended the weekend gathering.

At the moment, she stood talking with Laura Grant, the woman who owned the millinery next door to the accounting office. Percy, the young errand boy, had stormed into the shop with a package Laura had sent him to collect.

"I'm telling ya, me mum swears 'is Grace died of fright," he said with a shiver. "She said that there're ghosts of the people 'e wronged that went after 'im, and that if I don't do as she says, they'll come after me, too!"

"And do you believe that, Percy?" Vicky asked. "That a ghost who killed His Grace would go after you and hurt you in some way?"

Percy shook his head and adjusted the cap Vicky had given him for his birthday. "No, but it's fun to talk about it like it's true." He gave them a quick grin and bounded out of the shop, leaving the two women alone.

"It never ceases to amaze me the gossip that spreads through London," Laura said with a sigh. "But the boy is right. It is fun to listen to what people will believe."

Vicky laughed. "You are horrible!" she said. "Gossip is…well, it can be fun, but it also can be all too dangerous if one is not careful."

Laura smiled as she pulled back her blond hair and walked to the shop window.

The sun would soon set, and Vicky was growing hungry, but before she could excuse herself, Laura said, "Now, is that not an interesting sight? It appears that James is speaking with Molly Simpson."

Doing her best to walk when she wished to run, Vicky joined her friend at the window. Indeed, across the street stood Mr. Simpson, a client of theirs, standing with his daughter Molly. She was a pretty young woman with a yellow dress and matching hat that drew the eyes of several passing men.

"It won't be long before a woman catches his eye, you know," Laura said without turning. "And he will fall in love." She sighed. "It is odd, but he has seemed different since your return from the country. I'm not sure if his confidence has improved or… I don't know. It is difficult to place."

Vicky nodded, for she had seen the same changes in James. He no longer hid his hand or looked down at the ground when he spoke to others — men and women alike. The fact was, he was moving away from the man who hid himself away to a man who walked with his head held high and a grin on his face. And as Laura had said, he would soon find a woman with whom he could fall in love. A sharp pang in her breast made Vicky wince at the thought.

With a sense of urgency, she hurried to the shop door. "I will speak to you tomorrow," she said. "There is a path I must take, and I fear if I do not take it now, it will disappear."

Laura scrunched her brow in clear confusion. "I am unsure what you mean, but goodbye."

Most of the shops on the street had already closed for the evening as Vicky approached the trio. James gave Mr. Simpson a bow, and the man and his daughter walked away.

"James," Vicky called halfway across the street, "I would like to speak to you."

Meeting her halfway, he asked, "Is everything all right? You appear concerned about something."

"When we were at Stanting Estate and you saw me leaving Richard Kent's room, you told me that you knew I would one day find a man. You said that when that day came, you would be happy for me, but at the same time you would be sad."

"That is true," he replied. "If you have met someone, I only wish you the best. Both of you."

Vicky smiled as tears misted in her eyes. "I have met someone," she said. "A gentleman unlike any other in all of London. He is kind and caring, and I know that if I do not act now, I may lose him forever." She looked down at the cobblestones in an attempt to collect her thoughts. "I will not lie, I am terrified of being hurt again. I fear leaving the path I currently walk, for it has kept me safe for so long."

"I know what you mean," James said. "There is a sense of safety in closing off one's self."

Relief washed over Vicky. No one understood her like James did. "That is exactly what I mean. I would like to be honest with you. I must go slowly and use caution so I may explore these new feelings. But if you are willing to be patient with me, I would like you to join me on this new journey."

"You have no idea how long I have waited to hear you say these words," he said. "Yes, I would like nothing more in life than to join you and explore what can be. Together, we will walk this path to see where it may lead."

Vicky's heart soared, and she embraced James, not caring who witnessed it. Being in his arms felt right, comfortable, and safe.

When the embrace ended, she giggled as he handed her a handkerchief. "You always seem to know what I need when I need it," she said, sniffling as she dabbed at the tears that now filled her eyes. "Now, would you care to join me for dinner? I am famished."

"I would like that very much," James replied. He offered her his arm, and unlike the times before, Vicky did not hesitate to accept it.

And the two began to walk down a new path. Together, as one.

Printed in Great Britain
by Amazon